SONG OF A DETERMINED HEART

HEARTS OF ROARING FORK VALLEY

SARA BLACKARD

Copyright © 2023 by Sara Blackard

For more information on this book and the author visit: https://www.sarablackard.com

Editor Raneé S. Clark with Sweetly Us Press.
Cover designed by JS Designs Cover Art.

All rights reserved.

No part of this book may be reproduced in any form or by any electronic or mechanical means, including information storage and retrieval systems, without written permission from the author, except for the use of brief quotations in a book review.

This is a work of fiction. Names, characters, and incidents are all products of the author's imagination or are used for fictional purposes.

For PT
Thank you for providing me with the best name ever!

CHAPTER 1

◆

Klara Sorg swatted at the hay that tickled her neck. At least she hoped it was straw and not some six- or eight-legged pest she'd unfortunately become accustomed to. She wrinkled her nose at the smell coming from the horse in the stall next to her, the pungency causing her eyes to water. She'd have to remember to muck out the stalls tomorrow since it was obvious Hildebert Müller cared little for his animals.

A shiver skittered down her back, and it wasn't from the freezing cold or the hay. Too bad Hildebert didn't forget about her like he did his animals. He gave her more attention than she wanted. She shivered again and pulled the thin threadbare blanket tighter around her.

How in the world had she gotten here, sleeping in a barn so poorly built you could stand on one side and view the big mountain on the other? Where each night she found a different place to sleep in the small barn so a man nearly twice her age couldn't find her, a married man at that?

Oh, Vati, why'd you have to drag us here?

Klara closed her eyes and remembered the day her parents had approached her about their decision to travel west. She'd been playing the piano when they entered the parlor, her father smiling wide and her mother's gold rings clinking together as she wrung her hands.

"Mauschen, we've got some exciting news," her father had said. He'd always called her little mouse, though she was nineteen and far past marrying age. Of course, no one wanted a mute for a wife, so she supposed she'd always be "little mouse." "Klara, we have decided to venture west, to Colorado to be exact."

Colorado needed honest lawyers, and Vati wanted adventure. It didn't matter that Vati was one of the wealthiest men in Ohio. Once he set his heart on something, there was no stopping his determination.

The silver and gold boom popped up new towns left and right. Father had sent out scouts and found that the area called the Roaring Fork Valley on the western side of the Colorado Rocky Mountains showed promise. It wasn't as overrun as Leadville, but also not some place that would turn ghost town overnight. In fact, her father had believed it would be the perfect place to open his attorney office and start a new life.

Klara hadn't wanted a new life full of new people to turn their nose up at her. She begged him to change his mind. Why swap the comforts of the gilded life they had for an uncouth mining town? When he'd said God might have something good waiting in Colorado for her, she challenged him. God couldn't possibly have anything good in Colorado that she didn't already have in Ohio. She had been right. If only Vati had listened.

Klara stifled the sob that worked up her throat as she thought back to the arduous journey. Her father had hired another "good" German man whose family was also venturing out to Colorado to help them with the move. When they got off the train in Denver, the Müllers had been waiting for them.

Three days west over the mountains, Klara's parents had fallen sick. Bad water. Her mother died that night. Her father followed the next morning, but not before he passed her the small journal he wrote in daily. His whisper that the Müllers would help her still echoed in her ear. Would she even be able to find their hastily marked grave along the trail?

Klara realized very quickly the Müller's idea of help was more to their benefit than hers. She rubbed the callouses on her fingers and palms. She'd become less than a scullery maid, not only washing dishes and cleaning the house, but also scrubbing the laundry, gathering eggs, milking the cow, and mucking out stalls. The Müllers insisted she repay them for their troubles in bringing her to the Roaring Fork Valley and housing her, though Klara figured they'd gotten their pay in her family's belongings they'd either claimed as their own or sold.

Any time Klara spent catching her breath was quickly filled with another chore, usually accentuated with a slap on the face or a yank of the hair. She'd been called a stupid, worthless leech so many times, she wondered if it was true. Though Klara figured with the amount of time Maude sat reading her dime novels or buffing her nails, Maude held claim to that title more than Klara. Sure, Klara didn't know how to cook, but Maude spent such little time each day slapping food together for them that

Klara probably could figure out how to do that as well. However, Klara kept her thoughts to herself since she didn't want yet another chore added to her day.

The dry grass on the other side of the barn wall crunched with the weight of a foot. Klara froze and listened. Another heavy thump set her heart to racing. When the telltale sound of tobacco being spit signaled that Hildebert slunk toward the barn, her meager dinner curdled in her stomach. She buried herself deeper into the hay, curled into a tight ball, and squished her clamped knuckles to her lips.

From the moment her family first got off the train, Hildebert had stared at Klara in ways that had her pulling her shoulders in to hide herself, but his advances hadn't started until a week ago. At first, it had been a word in passing about how beautiful she was, "like Maude had once been." Then he had pulled a strand of hair that had fallen out of her bun through his fingers. Two nights ago, he'd started coming to the barn. She'd been able to hide without him finding her, but she wasn't sure how many more hiding spots she'd have before he'd have her cornered.

Now, she burrowed beneath the straw like some rodent hiding from a tom cat. The latch fumbled at the door. Klara squeezed her eyes shut, praying her shivering wouldn't give her away.

"Hildebert." Maude's voice snapped into the cold night air. "What are you doing out there?"

"I was just getting some fresh air. Thought I heard something in the barn." Hildebert's annoyed voice boomed loudly within Klara's ears.

"Of course, you heard something, you idiot. The barn

is full of animals. Get in here. It's time for bed." Klara wondered if Maude had always talked so harshly to her husband or if his wandering eyes had forced the tone.

Hildebert mumbled as he stomped toward the house. From his angered talking under his breath, Klara was thankful she couldn't understand the words. Her muscles relaxed with the slamming of the house door. Her sigh of relief into the smelly, dusty hay was quickly followed by silent sobs that wracked her body. Her father had been wrong. Colorado offered nothing but heartache and misery.

CHAPTER 2

Otto Lee pushed up from the dying campfire and breathed in the crisp morning air. Cupping the tin coffee mug in his hands, he closed his eyes and inhaled. The tangy smell of leaves beginning to display their final show of beauty before resting for the winter settled into his bones. He opened his eyes and marveled at Mount Sopris peeking through the tall trees.

Loud bleating overpowered the popping of coals, drawing his attention from the grand mountain to his pesky sheep. He chuckled and took a sip of his coffee. The sheep always seemed to know when the coffee finished boiling. Their bellowing would get more insistent with each sip he took.

They watched his morning routine of eating his fried salt pork and egg breakfast while the coffee darkened. The bleating would start low and soft, almost melodious, when he'd take his first bite of eggs from the fry pan. As he would take his pan to the small creek to wash it, the sheep would increase in volume like the murmurings of a crowd at the Fourth of July festivities back home in Kansas. By the time he got to the coffee, the fluffy rascals bleated away like the clanging of a hundred drums and blowing horns in discord. It was a good thing he had set up camp a ways off from Fryingpan Town, because the sheep's racket wouldn't endear him to any of the citizens of the growing town.

Duke, one of Otto's sheepdogs, sauntered up and sat at Otto's feet, observing the sheep. Duke glanced up at Otto, and Otto swore the dog cocked his eyebrow as if he agreed the sheep behaved ridiculously.

Otto laughed and bent down to rub Duke's side. "I know. They're contrary. You'd think we didn't let them graze at all yesterday."

Duke barked a short response.

"Yeah, I guess we should get going. They'll just get louder the longer we wait. Go ahead, Duke. I'll be right there," Otto said, taking another drink.

Duke trotted off on his three remaining legs, and Otto marveled once again at the amazing dog who had become his best friend. He couldn't believe how the dog had come back from the horrible accident last fall. It still turned Otto's stomach when he thought of Duke stepping into that wolf trap someone had hidden in the fall leaves.

Otto shuddered, the coffee turning sour in his gut. He tossed the rest of the drink into the dirt and got busy banking the coals so he could easily kick up the fire when he got back that evening. It wouldn't do him any good to ruminate on those horrifying memories when Duke's life had balanced so precariously. Duke would pick up on Otto's distress and not focus on the sheep like he should.

Otto saddled up Lemy, filled his canteen, and slipped

some jerky in the saddlebags. Leading Lemy toward the sheep, who sounded like an angry mob, Otto whistled his good morning song. He opened the gate to the sheepfold and greeted the woolies as they came out. He chuckled as they hoofed it toward the mountain meadow that spread before his camp. They pushed and shoved like St. Peter was about to close the pearly gates, and they didn't want to be left on the wrong side.

Baron, Otto's Great Pyrenees, walked regally out from the flock and sat before Otto. "How'd your charges do last night, Baron? Any trouble?"

Baron shook his head, his long white hair flying wildly with the motion. Laughter burst from Otto, his head falling back. He looked back down at Baron. The dog peered up at Otto as if his laughter was not appreciated. Baron huffed, then glanced at a sheep that was being extra pushy. With a heavy sigh, the giant dog lumbered over and walked beside the troublemaker, but first he threw Otto a look of long suffering. Supposedly, Baron was from a line of dogs first brought over by a French Marquis during the Revolutionary War. He had the attitude of royalty, that was for sure.

Otto followed the last of the flock, a smile twitching the corner of his mouth. The day stretched out long before him, but he was more content than he had ever been. When they reached the meadow, Duke took off with a yip after a younger sheep that had decided to wander a bit. Baron plopped onto the drying grass, his head high and alert as he guarded. Otto hobbled Lemy so he could graze and sat against a cottonwood to watch the sheep.

Duke jogged over to Otto, a grin on his face and his tongue hanging out. He flopped on the ground next to

Otto, panting hard. Where Baron scanned the flock in a slow, easy manner, Duke was the opposite, frantically moving his head from one place to the other, waiting for a charge to get out of their designated area so he could chase them down and put them back in their place. The personalities of the two dogs were as different as night and day, but without them, Otto wouldn't be able to succeed at sheep ranching by himself. Even with the dogs, he doubted he could.

He looked at the flock and shook his head. What in the world was Orlando Thomas thinking giving Otto five hundred sheep? Granted, the Thomas family was known throughout Colorado as having a blessed hand, but Orlando giving that much responsibility to Otto, a broken man he'd only met less than a year before, was downright loco.

Otto scuffed his boot in the dirt. Sure, Orlando hadn't actually given the sheep to him. Otto had signed the loan contract stating he'd pay Orlando back for the cost of the sheep, but Otto wondered if Orlando would cancel the loan when Otto failed and not require payment at all. He shook his head.

Otto had always struggled in school. He swapped numbers and letters, so his reading and sums weren't all that great. Yet, with his parents' encouragement, he'd pushed through and kept at school until he passed all the grades. Most he barely passed, but he passed nonetheless.

His pa had always wanted more for Otto than being a poor farmer on the plains of Kansas. He'd talk about Otto becoming something greater than his old man. When Otto's mother and younger sister had both died during an influenza outbreak, his pa had decided he wanted to be more than a poor farmer himself.

Otto knew it was just the heartbreak talking. His pa had always been proud of the farm he'd toiled up from nothing. Yet, with Otto's own heart torn in two, he hadn't put up much of a fuss when his pa had announced one day he was selling the farm and venturing west to find gold. Otto had been more than ready to leave the painful memories of death buried in the unyielding plains.

Yanking an old dandelion out of the dirt, Otto twirled the stem in his fingers. Wishes on a Stick, that's what his sister used to call the fluff. Even though he would scoff at her, he'd blown enough dandelion heads to be considered a fool. He tossed the dead flower down in disgust.

That wasn't the only reason he was a loggerhead.

His pa had decided to try Colorado on for size. Otto at first had questioned his father's assurances that he knew what he was doing. After three months of nothing but dirt and useless rocks, Otto had been yapping about pulling out and going to work for the mines. He still heard his father's words as if he sat right next to him.

"Son, most things in life are just like farming. The Good Book says that it don't really matter where you throw your seeds. As long as you have the Holy Spirit to guide you in your tossing, they'll grow fruit. So I'm throwing seeds of hope and dreams, having faith the Good Lord will sprout them."

Otto had scoffed at his father's declaration at the time, and still hadn't found in the Bible where God talked about that. Yet a week later, they were loading up their wheelbarrow with gold that seemed to push up from the dirt below the rocks like daisies.

Pa had sent Otto to Leadville to get the gold assessed.

His pa had warned him to stay clear of people and keep his head down. If only he had listened and kept his mouth shut.

If he had, Otto wouldn't have woken up in an alley stinking of alcohol and garbage, his pockets lighter than when he arrived. He wouldn't have come back to the mining claim in time to see his pa shot in cold blood by the men Otto had befriended in the saloon the night before. He wouldn't have fled in fear, leaving his father's body to the vultures.

No, no matter what Orlando or Otto's pa had thought, no matter how far God's forgiveness extended, Otto didn't deserve the blessing bleating before him. While his pa had thrown seeds of hope and dreams, Otto seemed only to throw seeds of failure. For Orlando's sake, Otto hoped God watered Orlando's seeds instead of Otto's. That was the only way this venture would succeed.

CHAPTER 3

Klara scrubbed the pan harder than necessary, ashamed she imagined that the stubborn, sticking eggs were Maude's face. Klara had noticed a gleam in Maude's eye that hadn't been there the night before. Maude had a curl to her lip that tainted her beautiful face.

Klara should've known the day would be worse than the one before. The birds sang much too cheerily, as if they wished to bolster her spirits for the morning to come. Klara touched her wet hand to her cheek that still stung from Maude's slap, then wiped the moisture away on her sleeve. Maude's demand that Klara make the eggs had been a surprise. The slap when the eggs turned out dry and almost burnt wasn't, though the ferocity of Maude's delivery still startled Klara.

Why had Maude insisted Klara cook when she knew Klara burned everything she came close to? Had she been waiting for an excuse to punish Klara? Klara shook her head and muttered "no" in her almost inaudible whisper she rarely let escape. Maude never seemed to need an excuse before. Klara's hand froze as a large clump of soggy, burnt eggs peeled from the pan. Had Maude taken her anger at Hildebert out on Klara?

Klara looked down and wondered what else she could do to minimize her appearance and dissuade Hildebert? She checked to make sure her hair was tightly wound in her bun and covered by the cloth swatch. She knew she didn't have to worry about her dress, since it now hung on her like a sack. She'd lost so much weight the last few months that both her remaining dresses fit so loosely they could squeeze two of her in them. She didn't understand how she could turn Hildebert's head when she looked more like a scrawny child with her small stature and now curveless body than a woman of nineteen.

Klara had to do something. She couldn't stay with the Müllers much longer if she wanted to keep what innocence was left to her intact. They may have stripped everything from her, but she refused to allow them to steal her virtue as well. However, she couldn't just take off without a plan. This was wild country, full of rugged miners, outlaws, and Indians.

Would the nice pastor that had stopped by when they first arrived help her? Maybe he could find a reputable place for her to stay and work until she could save enough to go back East. Would one of her aunts or uncles take her in? They'd never been very close since her father had moved them across the state of Ohio and then was too busy with his practice to visit. Surely at least one of her aunts or uncles would be willing to let her work for them in exchange for room and board? Anything would be better than the Müllers.

Klara went back to scrubbing the pan until all the bits

of burnt egg floated in the nasty dishwater. She hefted the heavy tub and turned to haul it outside and dump it in the garden. The delicate china teacup Maude had claimed from Klara's mother's belongings taunted Klara from the table. Klara's shoulders slumped. Sighing, she turned and put the tub back on the counter and retrieved the teacup from the table.

Klara turned the delicate china in her hand and remembered how much her mother had cherished the thing. It had belonged to the set Klara's grandmother had brought with her from Germany. Klara's grandmother had given each of her four daughters a delicate cup when they married, saying that a good sip of tea in a pretty cup could bring clarity to any situation. Klara's mother always said the best china was made by Frankenthal, and she'd turn the piece gently in her hand. Each time her mother had smiled at the pretty pink and yellow flowers and the marks marching down the handle, commenting on how they brought her so much joy, declaring Grandmother's claim proved true. Klara doubted the cup held much power anymore.

Klara brought it to the dishwater, peeking one last time inside the cup to the hidden flower bud on the bottom while she wiped a rebellious tear from her cheek. It'd do no good for her to cry now. She lowered the cup toward the tub only to groan in defeat. The greasy water with breakfast remains floating in it wouldn't do to clean the cup.

Or maybe it was the perfect water for it.

With a devious smile, Klara dunked the cup in the water, making sure to rub an extra large bit of egg around the rim. She swirled it in the rinse water and surveyed her work. She doubted Maude would notice any difference, but Klara would get a smidge of enjoyment out of the day. Maybe the birds' song had bolstered her, Klara thought with a small smile.

Klara grabbed the towel to dry the cup when a body suddenly pressed against her, pushing her sharply into the counter. Hildebert's tobacco-laced stench surrounded her as the teacup slipped from her fingers and crashed to the floor.

"Thought you'd be smart and hide from me?" Hildebert's harsh voice made Klara's body cold with dread.

He reached his hand around, splaying it upon her belly. Klara shook her head, her mind screaming for help. She tried to push back against him, but his bulk kept her pinned to the hard surface.

"You're so beautiful. You look just like Maude did before age and jealousy turned her ugly." He moved his hand upward and Klara tried to thrash to get away. He laughed. "The great thing about this is, if we're caught, I'll just tell everyone you seduced me. You can't tell people different. Besides, who would believe a stupid mute?"

He slid his hand inside the top of her dress. Klara bucked wildly and threw her head back. The whack of her skull against Hildebert's face sent stars to her eyes, but she didn't care since it also released Hildebert's hold on her. He bellowed in rage and pain. Klara turned around to dash out of the room. Hildebert clutched his face as blood ran between his fingers, just as Maude rushed in from outside.

"What in the wor—" Maude skidded to a stop, her eyes widened in alarm and bounced from Hildebert to Klara to the cup on the floor.

"She attacked me," Hildebert's stuffed voice yelled as he pointed a bloody finger toward Klara.

Klara's knees felt like they were about to give as she violently shook her head. She put up her hands as she backed toward the living room, not that the paltry gesture would stop Maude's advance.

"She threw your teacup at my face. I think she broke my nose." Hildebert sounded pathetic, but the gleam in his eye as he caught Klara's gaze dropped her throat into her stomach.

"You come into my house, take advantage of my hospitality, only to do this?" Maude's light blue eyes sharpened with each word she said.

Maude rushed forward, and Klara stumbled backwards. An almost silent scream opened Klara's mouth wide as Maude's palm slammed across the side of Klara's head, throwing her onto the floor. Maude pushed her knee into Klara's back, grabbing Klara by the hair.

"I see the way you're trying to steal my man." Maude threw Klara's face into the floor. "You're nothing but a thief, a halfwit, sneaky thief. I'll show you to steal from me."

Klara curled into a ball as Maude's foot connected to Klara's stomach. Her blood ran cold as she peered up and saw Hildebert's face and neck flushed with pleasure as he watched his wife kick Klara. She crawled for the front door. She had to escape this mad house, though she doubted anyone outside would care. She'd been woefully wrong the night before. Colorado held nothing but death for her.

CHAPTER 4

OTTO WHISTLED over Lemy's ears as he headed south into Fryingpan Town. Town was a loose term since the settlement consisted mainly of canvas tents pitched where the Roaring Fork and Frying Pan rivers converged, though a few buildings housed the mercantile and several saloons. The tents had started sprouting from the soil as soon as the Utes were all forced out earlier in the spring. Each time he came to town, he'd noticed a few new wooden buildings being slapped together. Would there be more dotted among the canvas?

Otto had spent the last fall and winter in the flattop mountains on the north side of the Grand River. It hadn't been too awful in the small, one room cabin he'd hastily stacked on a ridge overlooking the river. He had figured with the sentiments toward the Utes and the silver found in the area, his winter abode would be temporary, and he could move into the better lands that followed the Roaring Fork River to the Grand River.

His assumptions had been correct when the government cancelled the treaty with the Utes and had the tribes rounded up and driven like cattle west to Utah that spring. As soon as the dust had settled, he'd pushed the sheep down the mountain, found a good place to cross the Grand, and located a decent spread to stake a claim of land for the sheep. Though staking a claim was more an informal assertion than an actual purchase since he didn't have the funds yet to buy the property. He hoped since he set his camp further south from where the others were settling, he'd be all right for the time being.

He enjoyed the summer in the Roaring Fork Valley, where meadows laid abundantly between the surrounding mountains. He figured next summer the valley would fill up even more with miners once word spread that the land was clear to claim. If he did well enough with selling some of the sheep, he'd be smart to stake as wide a parcel as he could possibly get. With the way the land was formed, it wouldn't be long before farmers and ranchers alike showed up to lend their support to the local mines budding further up valley. He had one, maybe two more summers before his opportunity to get prime ranch land would be bust.

A horrid screeching pulled his attention out of his speculating. A tall blonde woman, her face red in rage, pulled on the hair of a smaller woman crawling across the yard. Otto flinched as the attacker kicked the woman in the stomach. He glanced around and didn't see any other people traveling close. This house had been vacant last time he'd been to town and sat a ways from the main town.

He looked back at the pair and noticed a man standing in the doorway of the house. His hands rubbed together, and an unkind smile stretched upon his lips as he watched the scene before him. Otto glanced again at the women and startled. The younger woman's bright blue eyes stared right at him, hope shining from her face, only to shutter into disappointment the longer he held her gaze. A slap across the woman's cheek broke their eye contact, causing Otto's breakfast to push up his throat.

He knew he should help, but the two looked like they could be family, either sisters or maybe even mother and daughter. Interrupting a family dispute would be highly unacceptable in the eyes of society but allowing a young woman to receive a beating in broad daylight, whether family or not, bordered on criminal to Otto's estimation. Hadn't Otto just read the story of the Good Samaritan in the Bible this morning? Granted the guy in that story had already been beaten to a pulp, but Otto didn't think God would approve of such violence as what played out before him.

Before he could think too much further, he gave a big yeehaw and charged Lemy up into the yard. The woman attacking startled at the interruption and stumbled backwards, giving Otto the opportunity to jump from his saddle and place himself between the two. The man stomped into the yard and placed his arm over the tall woman's shoulder who was still shaking and flushed with anger. His nose was swollen and bruised, and blood splattered his lip and shirt.

"Who do you think you are?" The woman's voice screeched high and loud.

"I'm the one stopping your unseemly treatment of this woman." Otto tried to put on a voice of authority he'd never used before, glad his tall, muscular stature stood above the man before him.

Out of the corner of his eye he noticed the little thing pushing to her knees and fumbling in her dress pocket. Her hair hung in disarray and red handprints marred both her cheeks that were wet with tears. Though she cringed and held her arm across her stomach, no sound came from her. This was either one tough cookie crumpled at his feet, or the attack had her in a state of shock.

"Unseemly treatment? Unseemly?" The older woman's escalating yells focused Otto's attention before him. "This woman is a wanton thief. Unseemly? She's nothing but dirt. A stupid mute who does nothing but laze about and thieve all day."

Otto glanced back as the lady pushed further up off the ground, shaking her head and grabbing his pant leg.

"What right do you have to interrupt personal family business, mister?" The man finally spoke, his tone condescending.

The injured woman shook her head more violently and wrote something in the dirt. Otto twisted his head to read. *Not family!*

"She says you're not family." Otto held the man's gaze, determined to help the injured woman one way or another. Family or not, this couple had no interest in her health.

"She's our servant." The man looked at the young woman, a gleam in his eye that caused the hair on Otto's neck to rise. "She owes us. Needs to pay us for our trouble."

Otto wasn't sure, but he swore the man's tone held desire in it. From the way the woman standing under the man's arm squinted up at her husband and the young woman's hand still pulling on Otto's pant leg shuddered, Otto didn't think he was wrong.

The older woman straightened and turned to Otto. "If you're so intent on sticking your nose where it doesn't belong, then you just claimed yourself the responsibility of dealing with the filthy thief. Me and my family are washing our hands of her." She lifted her chin, wrapped an arm around her husband's waist, and pulled him into the house. "Come on, Hildebert. She's not worth keeping around, the useless piece of dirt."

Otto crouched before the woman on the ground and gently laid his hand on her shoulder. She bowed her head, her shoulders shaking as silent sobs wracked her body. Otto's heart broke at the pain emanating from her.

"Miss, let's get you to the doctor." Otto moved his hand across her back to help her up.

She lifted her head, and blue eyes the color of the Colorado sky peered at him. Even with her golden hair pulled here and there from her bun and her cheeks red and tearstained, she was the most beautiful woman he'd ever laid eyes on. Her plush pink lips mouthed thank you as she spread her hand across the base of her throat.

"You're welcome." Otto swallowed the boulder stuck in his throat. "Let's get going."

He lifted her up into his arms and strode toward Lemy. She shook her head and pointed toward the barn. He took her in there instead, amazed when she hobbled across the filthy space and grabbed a bag stuffed deep under the hay. She nodded at him and walked toward the barn door. Her hand wrapped around her stomach without a backwards glance.

When he had her situated on the saddle, he mounted up behind her and clicked Lemy forward. She fumbled in her pocket, pulled out a stubby pencil and piece of paper, and wrote. Thankfully the message was short. *I'm Klara Sorg.* She looked at him with expectancy.

"It's mighty nice to meet you, Miss Sorg. I'm Otto Lee."

Klara beamed at him and bowed her head, wincing with the motion.

"Why don't you just relax back, Miss Sorg? It won't take long to get to town and get you looked at."

Otto prayed the doctor was still set up in the two tents he'd worked from all summer. He threw up another prayer for the little lady sitting ramrod straight in front of him. Mostly, though, he wondered what kind of mess he'd just charged in to.

CHAPTER 5

Klara gingerly pushed off the examination table of the nice doctor's office. Well, she supposed "office" was a bit of a stretch for the large canvas wall tent, but it was clean and had at least six beds for patients. She wasn't sure what was in the area through the back flap. Maybe there were more private rooms for patients or the doctor's residence?

She was glad there were no other patients there this morning to witness her wounds. It had been embarrassing enough having to show the doctor. She couldn't imagine doing so with others ogling.

Bruises already bloomed angrily around her midsection, but the doctor promised nothing was broken. He also promised she'd be in a lot of pain for the next week or so.

She slowly worked her way to the front of the tent, hoping to figure out something that would keep her away from the Müllers. She'd do anything not to have to see them again. Well, almost anything.

Klara stopped just inside the tent when she heard steady pacing footsteps and voices.

"Dan, I'm glad you're here. Maybe you can help figure out what to do with this young lady," Otto's urgent voice trumpeted outside. "I won't let her go back to that house. There was something evil lurking between that couple."

Klara's chest warmed at the determination in his voice. Had anyone ever cared so much about her well-being? Her father had, but Klara doubted her mother had. Her worry for Klara shifted to disappointment after the accident that had taken Klara's voice. Fresh tears smarted her eyes, and she quickly blinked them away. She was not going to be the weakling everyone thought she was.

"Are there any families in the area that would be willing to take her in?" An unfamiliar voice boomed through the thin fabric. Even though it was loud, its tone rang friendly.

"Not that I know of, at least none I would trust my daughter with," the doctor declared, and Klara's heart sank. "Fryingpan Town is still in its infancy, gentlemen. While it's grown exponentially the last few months, there are mainly miners and men tasked with providing for the miners here. Maybe by next summer we'll have more families, but she can't wait in the clinic until then."

Klara checked to make sure her small notebook and pencil were still in her dress pocket and squared her shoulders. If these kind gentlemen were going to plan out her future, she'd like to have a say in it. She pushed through the opening and stopped short when dark gray eyes filled with concern and a strong jaw with a cleft chin greeted her. *Otto.* His name breathed through her mind in a trill, and for once she was glad she couldn't talk.

Klara could have sworn that a knight in shining armor had ridden up to the Müller's earlier. She'd glanced up and seen a figure larger than life upon his valiant steed shadowed in the rising morning sun. Then he'd just stood there not moving, and Klara had figured her imagination had taken over her mind. The disappointment that had coursed through her had been shattering.

When he had charged onto the scene and stood between her and Maude, she'd almost fainted with relief. Now, if she didn't pull herself together, she'd faint for a whole different reason. A loud clearing of a throat snapped Klara out of her stare.

Otto shook his head, a light pink running up his tanned neck. "Miss Sorg, I'd like you to meet Trapper Dan. Dan, this is Miss Klara Sorg."

Trapper Dan pulled off his fur hat and bowed to Klara, giving her a good view of his wild red hair. "It's a pleasure to meet you, Miss Sorg. I hear you find yourself in a conundrum."

Klara nodded, glancing between the three men. Doctor Jones pushed his spectacles up to his graying eyebrows. Otto bobbed his head, his hand rubbing his cleft chin in what looked like concentration. Trapper Dan looked between her and Otto, and a large smile bloomed upon his face.

"Yet, I think what we've got is divine intervention." Trapper Dan slapped Otto on the back.

"What are you talking about?" Otto's eyebrows scrunched over his dark eyes.

"Well, look here. You're a nice, young man with a future in ranching here in these fine meadows. Miss Sorg is a pretty young woman who needs a home and family." Trapper Dan pointed between Otto and her.

Klara felt her eyes widening in mirror fashion as Otto's did. Was this crazy man suggesting what she thought he was?

"Are you suggesting we get ... get married?" Otto sputtered.

Klara glared at Otto and his shocked tone. What would be so horrible about marrying her?

"We don't even know each other!" Otto flung his hands wide.

Well, there was that. Klara conceded and relaxed her face. Some other plan could be thought up.

"Miss Sorg doesn't seem against the idea. She hasn't spoken a word of complaint." Trapper Dan motioned toward her like Otto should be paying attention.

"That's because she can't. She's ... she's—" Otto stuttered and rubbed his neck, making Klara wonder what he wanted to say but didn't.

"Miss Sorg had a type of surgery called a tracheotomy when she was younger." Doctor Jones patted her on the arm. "When a swarm of bees attacked and her airway closed off, she was cut in the throat so she could breathe until the swelling went down. It's not a widely used practice, and unfortunately in Miss Sorg's case, her voice box was damaged during the procedure."

Otto's eyes went wide, and his face paled. "Someone cut your throat?"

Klara appreciated the concern in his voice over the stuttering.

"It's all right, young man." Doctor Jones chuckled. "She is quite fine now."

"She might be a mute, but she's mighty pretty." Trapper Dan grinned at Klara, causing her to blush in embarrassment. He turned to Otto and smiled bigger. "Besides, a mute wife might just be a blessing."

Klara's mouth swung open. The warmth of embarrassment on her cheeks turned to the heat of anger. How dare he?

Otto stood up straighter. His arms dropped to his side, and his hand clenched and unclenched.

"She's mute, Dan. Not deaf." Otto took a menacing step closer to Trapper Dan. "You better watch your tongue around her."

Klara's heart picked up its pace like a staccato melody. No one, not even her father, had publicly defended her in such a manner. Of course, back home no one would've dared say such a thing about Alf Sorg's daughter in his presence, no matter how secluded she stayed.

Trapper Dan held his hands up in surrender. "I meant no disrespect, Otto, I promise." Trapper Dan shrugged. The melancholy look that touched his face was quickly replaced by a soft grin. "Besides, what do I know? I'm just an old bachelor who spends more time with the porcupines than people." He turned to Klara and put his hand over his chest. "Please forgive me if I offended you. I honestly meant no disrespect."

Klara put her hand over her heart and bowed her head in acceptance. Even though the compliment about her being pretty was off-handed, she liked the rough man. He had a handsome face hidden beneath the bushy, auburn beard and wild hair. Why had such a nice, good-looking gentleman never found a wife? He seemed all-fired for someone else to get married but hadn't himself.

"Listen, all joking aside." Trapper Dan looked around.

Klara stood up straighter and glanced around the makeshift town. A wagon rumbled by with a couple of rough looking men sitting on the bench. One with a chewed-up cigar opened his mouth and laughed boisterously, showing his blackened teeth. Another man stumbled out of a tent further down the road, tripped on his feet, and went sprawling in the dirt. Loitering men pointed and roared with laughter, but no one assisted the man up.

All around her, life clanged and clattered, setting her nerves to buzzing like an orchestra tuning up before a grand symphony. The Müllers hadn't allowed her to come to town. Aside from when they first arrived, she didn't truly understand the situation she was in. She wanted to rush back into the doctor's tent and hide but knew that cowardice wouldn't change her circumstance.

"Our options are limited," Trapper Dan continued. "Like Doc said, there aren't going to be any families coming in soon, especially with winter threatening in the mountains already. No one will be trekking over the divide to Denver, either." Trapper Dan stared at Klara steadily, comforting her in a way she didn't think possible. "I don't think I'd like to send our Miss Sorg off to Denver with any of these yahoos, anyways."

Klara peeked at Otto. He paced away and rubbed the back of his neck. He paced back, his shoulders slumped.

"Dan, I've got nothing but a bunch of sheep, a couple of dogs, and a wall tent for a home." Otto's voice strained with an emotion Klara couldn't place. "I've nothing to offer her."

An objection rose into her heart, but Klara quickly

stuffed it down. She didn't know Otto. So why did the self-deprecation in his voice rile her?

Trapper Dan stepped close to Otto, halting his pacing with a fatherly hand on the shoulder. "That's not true, son. You're a strong man who can offer her protection, and a godly man who won't take advantage."

Otto shook his head, his whisper almost too low to hear. "Dan, you know my past, my cowardice."

"Son, everyone has a past." Trapper Dan put his arm around Otto's shoulder and led him away a few paces. Trapper Dan's voice pitched low, but Klara could still hear enough to catch a word or two. "What happened ... father wasn't...fault."

"I should've..."

Klara had to strain hard to hear Otto speak.

Trapper Dan shook his head. "Then ... been killed, too."

Klara jerked at the declaration, wondering what horrible thing had happened to Otto and why it seemed he blamed himself. Klara stopped trying to listen to their conversation and closed her eyes. What should she do?

It was obvious Otto didn't want her as a wife, so shouldn't she convince them there was a different option? She wasn't even sure she wanted to be Otto's wife. She had to admit his handsome face with its cleft chin and stormy eyes wouldn't be a hardship to look at through the years. A handsome face was not reason enough to marry a total stranger, though. She'd never been like the spoiled girls her mother had forced her to share tea with, who cared more about a roguish grin and the wave of golden hair than the character of their beau.

What other options were there to her? Her chances of

getting over the mountains to Denver and catching a train back to Ohio seemed slim to none. At least with company that would keep her virtue intact. Besides, she didn't even know if her family would take her in. None of them had ever exchanged even a note of inquiry with her parents before they'd left Ohio, something her mother had complained about repeatedly under her breath when she was upset at Klara's father for one thing or another.

"Miss Sorg?"

Otto's deep, smooth timbre entered Klara's thoughts. She took a slow breath in and opened her eyes. The other two men had moved some paces away and were conversing. Not that she really noticed or cared with Otto standing a mere foot in front of her. His hands tortured his wide-brimmed hat he held before him, revealing dark blonde hair that tucked behind his ears and flopped onto his forehead. It wasn't long and stringy like a lot of the men she'd seen today, but definitely needed a trim.

His clean-shaved face turned slightly pink as he cleared his throat and peered into her eyes. "Miss Sorg, I know we just met and circumstances aren't ideal, but if you are willing, I'd like to offer my name and home, be it what it is, in marriage."

A groan issued from Trapper Dan as he turned away and shook his head. Klara smothered the grin that threatened to turn her lips upward. As proposals went, Otto's proposal lacked luster.

Could she really bind herself to a man she didn't even know? What kind of man would willingly marry a mute? No one had ever given her more than a glance in passing, dashing Klara's hopes of family and children of her own into the ground. Yet here in the wilderness of Colorado, a man had just asked for her hand, in a manner of speaking.

"Not that we'd actually have to be married in that way ... I mean, we wouldn't have to act like a married couple." He groaned and rubbed his neck that grew more crimson with each word. "What I'm trying to say is that we wouldn't have to consummate our marriage. Ours would be for your protection, but I wouldn't want to do that ... that is, take advantage. Grrr."

Otto's words came out in an awkward, halting rhythm, like a novice attempting a complex musical score.

"Just stop while you're ahead," Trapper Dan whispered loudly from where he stood, then turned to Doctor Jones. "Not that he's ahead in the first place."

Klara inwardly giggled at the same time as her heart slightly broke, which was utterly ridiculous. Klara understood marrying her benefited Otto in no way. It was juvenile to believe he wanted to marry her more than simply for her protection. Stuffing down her disappointment, she reached out and touched Otto's arm. When he glanced into her eyes, she nodded and smiled encouragement.

"Yes?" Otto asked hesitantly.

Klara nodded again and mouthed thank you to show her appreciation for his sacrifice. Otto sighed, and his face stretched into a tremulous smile. She worried he sighed in acceptance rather than relief. Cold rushed through her and caused her to shiver. Why had she agreed to sacrifice this nice man's life and hope for a true marriage just to save herself?

CHAPTER 6

Otto tried to listen as Trapper Dan spoke the words binding him to the beautiful woman standing beside him. He truly did. Yet, the moments that had led him to standing before Trapper Dan in a wedding ceremony that was not someone else's but his own kept flashing through his head. He could honestly say this was not something he'd ever considered could happen as he commanded the dogs to guard the sheep and mounted Lemy that morning.

The old timers all said one had to be prepared for anything in the Rocky Mountain wilderness. Otto always assumed that meant grizzly attacks or being stalked by a mountain lion, not having a wife plopped onto your lap. Though having Klara on his lap was a surprise he could honestly say he wouldn't mind. She was a lot better looking and nicer smelling than a grizzly, to his way of thinking. Otto blushed at the direction his thoughts had taken him and peeked to make sure Klara hadn't read his mind.

Klara turned her clear blue eyes to him and smiled.

The light sky-colored fabric of the ready-made dress he'd bought her at the one and only store made her eyes so blue he swore he'd never seen anything as pretty. They reminded him of the alpine forget-me-nots he'd found in the rocky slopes earlier this summer, all full of guarded hope. He'd been tempted to pick them until one of the sheep had torn them up from the dirt for lunch. The thought pulled his eyebrows together. Would he end up yanking out that hope he saw banked in Klara's eyes, just like that sheep had ripped those flowers from the ground?

Klara's forehead crinkled in concern, and Otto quickly smoothed his face and smiled at her. A sheen filled her eyes before she blinked it away and turned toward Trapper Dan. Her shoulders slumped slightly. Otto ground his teeth at his idiocy. If he could hit himself over the head, he would, and from the expression Dan pointed his way, Otto wouldn't be the only one whacking.

What kind of fool scowled at his wedding? It wasn't like he was opposed to marrying Klara. Well, he supposed he was but only because of his own lack of character and nothing to do with the woman beside him. She was honest to goodness the most beautiful thing he'd ever laid eyes on. Though she couldn't voice words, her expressions spoke volumes. Otto hoped in time he could translate them. What was he doing strapping her to a coward like himself? She deserved to marry someone of honor, someone who didn't run out on their family and leave justice unclaimed.

"I now pronounce you husband and wife." Trapper Dan boomed to the small crowd that had formed to watch the impromptu ceremony in front of the doc's tent. "You may kiss the bride."

Cheers went up as Otto stared at Trapper Dan. Otto had told Dan to skip the whole kissing part. A pretty blush dusted Klara's ears as she lowered her gaze to the ground.

Otto leaned in and placed a soft kiss on her hot cheek, and a sweet, slightly medicinal smell entered his nose and filled his senses. He moved away before he did something even more idiotic, like claim her lips that were parted slightly in surprise. He'd promised her their marriage would be one of convenience, and he was going to hold true to that promise, come hell or high water. He just hadn't realized it would be a difficult promise to keep.

Otto reached down and tentatively grabbed her hand. It shook like a golden aspen leaf preparing to fall. He gave it a squeeze.

When she peered up at him, he smiled. "Don't worry, Klara. You'll be safe with me."

Hope flashed back in her eyes. She nodded and turned to the doctor who had approached. Otto prayed his words would hold true.

Trapper Dan clapped him on the shoulder. "I'm heading into the mountains in the next day or two to check on some friends, but I plan on swinging by before I head out. I might have something I'd like to run by you, but I'd like to do some investigating first."

"All right." Otto's mind reeled with questions.

He didn't have a clue what Trapper Dan could possibly need to run by him. Otto shrugged. There was no use fretting over a conversation that might not happen. He gave Trapper Dan directions to his home as he led Klara to the hitching post.

Otto had already loaded the saddlebags with the

supplies he had picked up at the store, including some frilly items that hadn't been on the list that morning at breakfast. Sweet smelling soap, a purple dress with lace along the collar, and the blue dress that made his wife's eyes pop hadn't even existed in his brain before. Who the paltry supply of women's items was stocked for Otto couldn't say, but he was glad to get Klara out of the shapeless sack she'd been wearing.

Otto rubbed the back of his neck. He'd have to watch himself and his pockets more closely on future trips. Not because he put an ounce of worry into what those polecats had said about Klara, but because every bit of fancy he'd seen on those limited shelves he'd wanted to give to her. His modest funds would dwindle faster than spring grass with a flock of sheep if he kept it up.

Otto grabbed Klara's small waist, his hands finding bones where meat should be. Did those varmints starve her as well? He'd have to make sure she ate well and fattened up, otherwise she would freeze come winter. Of course, there were other ways to stay warm. Otto ground his thoughts to a halt and lifted her carefully into the saddle.

"Mrs. Lee, it's been a pleasure. You sure have made my day joyful." Trapper Dan beamed up at her.

Otto's surname attached to her startled her as much as it did him if the look on her face proved honest. Quickly following the surprise rushed a warmth he hadn't expected. He rubbed his chest and cleared his throat, turning to the doctor.

"Thank you, Doc. Are you sure we don't owe you anything?" Otto shook the kind doctor's hand.

"No, no. It's my wedding gift to you, such as it is." He

turned his gaze up to Klara. "Now dear, you make sure you take it easy the next few days. Those bruises are going to smart."

Klara's face turned red as she nodded and glanced at Otto. The thought of what her skin must look like after the beating burned hot in his gut. Trying not to bump her body, he mounted up behind her before he did something he'd regret, like handing down some frontier justice to the Müllers. Just as God wouldn't have wanted Klara treated like she had been, God didn't want the Müllers to suffer what was running through Otto's head. In fact, from what he'd ciphered out of the Bible, God didn't even appreciate Otto's direction of thoughts.

Vengeance will be mine, saith the Lord.

All right, Lord. Otto would leave vengeance up to Him.

Otto may be able to leave the Müllers to the Lord to deal with, but he wasn't sure he could wrangle in his heated thoughts. He'd just have to spend a lot of time in prayer to turn his contemplations to God and set his mind on the right track.

As Lemy stepped off down the road, Klara leaned into Otto. Her back curved softly into his chest, and Otto knew he'd be praying for more than just justice against the Müllers. He might break down heaven's door with prayers of help to become a man who honored his word to his tempting new wife. No old-timer had ever prepared him for what sat before him.

CHAPTER 7

Klara woke with a start as the horse neighed loudly in front of her. She sat up straight, only to wince back into the chest that held her. Somehow, she had ended up sitting sideways in the saddle, strong arms holding her in place.

"Now, look what you did, Lemy. You startled the poor lady." The calm timbre of her husband's voice settled into her bones.

Settled that is, until she remembered she had a husband she hadn't even known of a few hours before. She sat back up more slowly this time and tucked the loose strands of her hair that blew into her face behind her ear. An almost inaudible sigh came from beside her. She peeked to see if she could tell if the sound came out of relief.

Otto's gray eyes stared back at her. Contentment reflected in the smoky color. She breathed more easily, glad regret didn't mar her handsome husband's face.

Otto smiled, and warmth rushed to Klara's gut. "Sorry the lug startled you awake."

Klara shrugged, and Otto smiled larger, a twinkle in his eye. "You know, I was just thinking. It's not every day you go into town to grab some flour and salted pork and come home with a wife. I wonder what will be waiting for me next time I venture in?"

Laughter silently rushed from Klara. She covered her mouth to hide her teeth, knowing her mother would've been appalled by the display.

"Now, Klara … can I call you Klara?" Otto lightly gripped her fingers as she nodded. "Why would you hide such a cheerful sight?" He pulled her fingers from her mouth and smiled. "Seeing your laughter is like sunshine after a cloudy day." Otto chuckled and shook his head. "Marriage done turned me into a poet."

Klara peeked up at him and offered a small smile. She then looked at how she was sitting and motioned her arms to him. She hoped she wouldn't have to dig out her notepad. Writing while on the back of a horse might prove cumbersome.

"How'd you end up sideways?" Otto asked, and Klara nodded at his question. "Well, when you fell asleep, you just about toppled off Lemy's back, so I tucked you in against me, and you settled right down."

Klara gaped at him, her mouth opening and closing. She hadn't slept so soundly since leaving Ohio and definitely not since arriving here, where she had to constantly be on guard. How had she fallen asleep so deeply that she had almost fallen off the horse?

What was it about this man that made her trust him? She probably shouldn't have confidence in that trust, not after the hard lessons she'd been dealt over the last months, but she was exhausted from always being on edge. She would pull on her mantle of suspicion when her body and mind didn't weigh so much.

Klara snapped her mouth closed and mouthed that she was sorry.

"It was no problem at all, Klara. What with you such a teeny bit of nothing, you were easy to hold." Otto shrugged and looked around uncomfortably. "I'm glad you slept."

She placed her hands to her mouth and moved them away while mouthing thank you. His gaze dropped to her lips as he watched them intently.

He smiled and moved his attention up to her eyes. "You're welcome."

She pointed to the horse and mouthed Lemy, making sure to scrunch her face in a questioning expression.

"My pa always wanted me to be more than just a Kansan farmer, so he bought any book the store got in that wasn't a dime novel." Otto shrugged. "Ptolemy was Alexander the Great's closest bodyguard and advisor. The name always stuck with me, and since most of my talking out my problems happens in the saddle, seemed like a fitting name for my faithful friend."

A loud ruckus drew her attention to the trees up ahead. She couldn't see what was making such an awful noise, but whatever it was had to be monstrous. She hated that her body began to shake. Otto groaned, then started chuckling a low sound she almost missed over the racket. She turned her startled expression from scanning for danger to him.

"You'll have to excuse the sheep. They're a little cranky

I left them in the sheepfold for the morning." A look of fondness belied the cantankerous tone in his voice.

Klara found herself repeating the word sheep. She peered under the brush and through the trees for some massive beast sheep hiding out. Certainly, the horrible noise couldn't come from the fluffy pictures she'd seen in nursery books.

"They're demanding as all get out. I'll walk us by the sheepfold so you can see them before I take you home." Otto sighed a different sigh than earlier causing Klara to stop her searching for the sheep and survey Otto's expression.

She didn't understand what she saw.

"Listen, Klara. I probably should have warned you more, shouldn't have let Dan goad me. The thing is, I don't have much but a bunch of sheep, a tent, and another man's dream. I can't even claim it as my own." Otto gave a short, harsh laugh and looked out over the mountains. "A friend of mine wanted to test out whether sheep ranching could work here in Colorado, so he bought up a bunch of sheep, some dogs, and gave half to me."

Klara's eyes went wide in question. Why would anyone just give sheep away? She cocked her head and waved one hand for him to continue.

"Well, I guess he didn't give them to me, but I took them out on loan. He said it was an experiment that might not work and wanted to give the cranky beasts to me, but we agreed on a loan amount that I pay him over time as the sheep sell."

Otto got that far-off look again as he rubbed his neck, something she noticed he did when he was nervous. She kept her hands placidly in her lap, though she wanted to cross them over her chest. She was glad she sat upon the horse, otherwise, she'd be tapping her toe in impatience.

"Anyway, I've doubled my sheep count since I got them last fall. If I can just figure out the business side of it, I think it will be profitable. We might not make it rich like the silver miners do, but we won't be scraping by, either. That is, once I figure out how and where to sell them without depleting the flock too much."

Something sparked in Klara when he said "we." She patted Otto on the chest in what she hoped was encouragement. She smiled and nodded at him, too tired to take the time to dig out her paper and write an encouragement. So, she'd married herself a sheep rancher? What exactly that entailed, she hadn't a clue.

As they cleared the trees, the bleating got so loud she covered her ears. Sheep milled around an enclosure. There had to be at least five hundred or more. She turned to Otto and pointed to her fingers as if she counted.

"There's around nine hundred sheep, well nine hundred twenty-six sheep to be exact." Otto scratched his head. "We had a lot of twins this spring."

Klara nodded her head slowly, not even knowing how one knew the exact count of sheep when they reached that high of a number. Otto turned the horse from the bleating animals and headed toward a tent set up under a grove of aspens. A creek ran close to the camp.

It was a good thing she couldn't talk, because there wasn't much to be said about her new home other than it sat in a pretty spot. The tent looked solid enough, at least as far as tents went, but couldn't be bigger than an eight-foot square. She wondered how they would stay warm during the winter, then blushed at the thought of the strong arms wrapped around her at that moment heating her through the winter as well. She couldn't be thinking like that when he'd made it abundantly clear he wasn't interested in such things.

Her lips formed a pout which she quickly replaced with a smile. The poor man had already sacrificed his freedom for her. She wasn't about to slap him with a petulant wife to rub salt in his wounds. She turned her gaze to him and gave him a look she hoped showed her gratitude. She'd do whatever she could to prove she wasn't worthless and make this marriage easier for Otto. She wasn't exactly sure how, but she'd spend a good amount of time asking God for inspiration.

A bird trilled a happy song from its perch in the aspen trees above. Another answered in kind from behind the tent. Klara closed her eyes and relished the light-hearted feeling she hadn't experienced since her father had announced they were moving. Maybe the birds' song this morning wasn't to bolster Klara for the horrendous day ahead, but a premonition of the relief God would bring to her in the form of one tall, chiseled-faced stranger. Klara thanked God for the hopefulness that fluttered through her chest and made her fingers tingle.

CHAPTER 8

OTTO STARED up at the blinking stars as the moon made its dash across the dark sky. The moon, large and gleaming, illuminated the camp brightly and reflected off the stream in brilliant ripples. The babbling of the creek and *chirrups* of the crickets rolled the tension from this morning's encounter off his shoulders like the water over the rocks.

A soft breeze picked up, swirling the smoke of the fire up and causing Otto to pull his coat tighter around his shoulders. A coyote yipped in the distance, the only sound in a quiet night that should be lulling Otto to sleep. Yet, he couldn't cross the few feet to the tent.

After Klara had almost fallen asleep standing when they arrived home, Otto had suggested she lie down. She'd only gotten up twice. Once for the necessary and again for dinner, where she ate little.

Every time he'd checked on her, she'd been rolled tightly into a ball, her even breath softly blowing. She'd looked so vulnerable and scared, even in sleep, that Otto had been mighty tempted to ride out to the Müllers and give them a piece of their own medicine. He'd also been tempted to crawl in there, pull her close, and tell her she could relax now that she was with him, which had frightened him. He had no business thinking like that.

He pushed his hand through his hair. Otto wouldn't readily admit he was afraid of going in the tent, but every time he thought of turning in, his heart raced, and his palms slicked with sweat. Maybe he should sleep by the fire tonight.

The wind whipped around him, kicking sparks up from the flames and knocking the coffeepot over. Otto rushed to the pot and set it in his storage box, placing the lid firmly on it. Another gust of wind almost snatched his hat.

He gazed east and saw nothing but black. A flash of lightning shot through the sky, followed by a distant rumble. There'd be no sleeping outside tonight, not unless he wanted to get drenched.

He rushed to the sheepfold and found them all sleeping through the storm. Duke greeted him with a sharp, happy bark. Otto bent down and gave the dog a good pat.

"You keep watch tonight, all right? Keep watch." The dog leaned his head into Otto's rub, then took off for the sheepfold as Otto hurried back to the tent.

Otto hustled to put everything else away that might get ruined by the rain or blown away and doused the fire so the wind wouldn't blow any sparks into the drying grass. Though it'd probably rain and put out the flames, he didn't want to risk a wildfire if it just decided to blow.

He ducked into the tent and tied the flap closed. He was crawling onto his bedroll when Klara attacked him like a wildcat with a solid slap to the side of his head that left his ears ringing. Quick breaths and hands and feet connecting with him were all he heard. A hard thrust to his stomach whooshed all the air from him. Maybe Klara hadn't needed his help after all this morning.

"Klara, it's me. Settle down now." As gently as he could, he wrapped her arms against her body so she didn't hurt herself anymore. She jerked, trying to get free, and Otto worried he'd hurt her. "It's Otto. Klara, sugar, stop. I'm not going to hurt you."

She froze. Her breath sounded ragged and quick in the space between them. She trembled, and he loosened his grip and rubbed his hands up and down her arms.

"It's me, Otto. You're okay." He kept his words soft like he talked to one of his frightened sheep. "I promise. I'm not going to hurt you."

She lifted her hands, patting them up his shirt to examine his face. Her exhale shuttered out as she collapsed into his chest. The wind attacked the side of the tent as silent sobs heaved her shoulders. She clutched his shirt in her small hands.

Otto tentatively wrapped his arms around her, praying she'd find comfort. Her body was stiff beneath his hands. His throat closed as if someone had tightened a noose. How was he to ever help this wife of his? She was broken, and he hadn't the foggiest clue what to do. He hadn't been able to help his ma and sister when they'd gotten sick. He certainly hadn't helped his pa when those claim jumpers killed him. Smarts had never graced him. He'd probably ruin Klara like he had everything else.

Klara pulled back and pushed against his chest. He instantly dropped his hands and leaned back to give her space. He felt her bring her knees into her chest as she scooted away from him. He hated that he couldn't see her, couldn't read her expressions to know how she felt. He pulled a match from his pocket and lit the lantern that hung from the tent ceiling. From the corner of his eye, he saw her head on her knees as she took deep breaths and sniffled.

Otto sat back on his heels at a loss as to what to do. He closed his eyes, hung his chin to his chest, and prayed. What would he do if it was his sister sitting here, frightened and in pain? He knew exactly what he'd do, but would it help? He took a deep breath and scooted next to Klara.

"Klara, are you alright?" He ran his hand gently over her hair like he remembered his mother doing when he was a child.

Klara lifted her head. Her red-rimmed eyes made the blue brighter. Otto's heart twisted at her blotchy skin against the swollen and bruised cheeks. His eyes teared up, and he quickly blinked the moisture away.

"Are"— He cleared the rock from his throat.—"Are you okay?"

Klara nodded. She motioned that she'd been asleep. She opened her eyes and acted like she couldn't see. Then, she motioned to the walls of the tent and what he thought might be wind. When she pointed to him, then moved her hands in front of her so they opened wide and her eyes got big.

"I'm sorry I scared you." Otto sat back and ran his

hand over the back of his neck. "I should've known the storm would wake you. I wasn't thinking, not letting you know it was me coming in."

She shook her head and lifted her hand in front of her and mouthed 'Okay.' Otto realized just how much her not being able to talk was going to make their marriage hard.

He inwardly chided himself. Whatever challenge her lack of voice presented, they'd figure it out. He had no room to whine, even if it was only in his head. With that, he set out to make his new wife comfortable. Well, as comfortable as one could be in a tent during a raging storm with a complete stranger.

"There's a doozy of a storm blowing in."

Klara's eyes darted to the tent's sides.

"Don't worry. I've set the tent up to last the winter. It's sturdy, and I've placed it on a platform. So we should stay nice and dry." Unless the creek flooded, but he wasn't going to bother her with that information.

The wind whipped the flap open, gusting air through and making the lantern sputter and threaten to go out. Otto jumped to the flap and tied it tight. Slumping in the short ceiling, he scanned the two trunks lined on one side and the two wool-blanketed pallets inches apart in the rest of the space. When he'd left that morning, he'd had a nice walkway down the middle, but sleeping pallets for an extra person took up all the extra space. He straightened the bedding that had blown cattywampus in the wind. Klara flinched as she bent to help.

"It's all right, Klara. I've got this." Otto patted her softly on the shoulder. "Doc said you were to take it easy."

Klara slumped and crossed her arms. Her eyes

narrowed before she looked away. Otto wondered what he'd done wrong to make her so mad. He was just trying to keep her from aggravating her injuries more than she probably already did with her wild attack minutes ago. The wind shook the tent again, causing the lantern to throw chaotic shadows to dance upon the tent walls.

Klara's wide eyes whipped to his. She mouthed something, drawing Otto's attention to her lips. Her very kissable, pink lips. Otto shook his head to clear his thoughts. Klara huffed and mouthed the word again.

Sheep?

"The sheep?" Otto marveled at how she'd worry about the animals over herself. "They'll be fine. The sheepfold will keep them penned and safe. When they're all bunched up like that, not much but a wolf pack howling will upset them."

She wrung her hands as she nodded. Glancing around the tent, her gaze lingered on her pallet. She yawned, then quickly hid it behind the back of her hand.

Sorry. She cringed and shrugged.

"Don't apologize. I'm tuckered out, too." Otto smiled. "Why don't you get settled, and then I'll turn the lantern off."

Klara nodded and quickly wiggled into her bedroll. She tucked her hands beneath her cheek and closed her eyes. Otto took a minute to straighten out his bedding, placing his revolver next to where his head would lay. He glanced one last time at Klara. Though her bruised face broke his heart, she looked at peace as she lay there. She hadn't curled into the tight ball he'd seen her in every time he'd checked on her earlier that evening. He prayed she'd stay relaxed througout the rest of the night.

Otto blew out the lantern and made his way to his bed. He tried keeping his pride in check that his presence gave her the sense of protection needed to sleep peacefully. If history had any say in the matter, she'd probably lose trust in him like everyone else had.

CHAPTER 9

Otto took a deep breath, pushing down his embarrassment as he stepped from the tent to greet Trapper Dan. The mountain man's hollered greeting had jerked Otto awake. He hadn't meant to oversleep. Hadn't thought he'd sleep at all with the distraction of his wife next to him.

His wife.

He swallowed down his smile and shook his head. Didn't matter how late he'd lain awake marveling at her relaxing close to him shortly after she fell asleep. The storm had shaken the canvas for hours, but she hadn't flinched or woken. In the darkness of night, all kinds of imaginings raced through his head, mostly centered around her trust in him. Even if it was only when she wasn't awake.

Didn't matter that he'd hardly slept. He should've been up long ago, and now he got caught being lazy by one of the few men who had encouraged him to do better. From the smug look dancing in Trapper Dan's eyes, there'd be no hiding the fact it was well past sun-up, and Otto had just rolled out of bed.

"Morning," Otto lifted his hand in greeting, then bent over the campfire to move the wet wood out of the way.

"And a fine morning to you." Dan didn't even try to hide the chuckle in his voice.

Otto ignored the heat racing up his neck making it hotter than any sunburn he'd had. He clenched his teeth as he flicked the soaking wood off to one side. With all the coals thoroughly doused, he'd have to find some dry wood to build the fire up again. He hadn't even checked the sheep yet, though their low murmurs said they were fine. There was too much to do to sit around chatting, but he couldn't be rude to the man who had helped him take the steps back to himself.

"I'd offer you coffee, but it'll be a bit before it's done." Otto strode to the base of the tree where he stored the firewood and searched the bottom of the pile for any dry pieces, snatching his hatchet from the limb it hung on.

"Oh, I've had my fill of coffee already, but thanks." Dan swung off his horse and scanned the homestead, if a tent and sheepfold could be called that.

As Otto carried the wood back to the fire pit, the flap on the tent pushed back. Klara cringed as she stepped out, her arm wrapping around her middle. Otto dropped the wood and hatchet and rushed to her side.

"Klara, you shouldn't be up." He wrapped his arm around her tiny waist and took her hand to lead her back inside.

She shook her head, her free hand motioning. The blue dress he'd bought her the day before hung loose on her, and she leaned into him more than she had when he'd first brought her home. When she gazed up at him with pleading in her eyes, he knew he'd give in.

"The doc said you're supposed to rest," he whispered low to her, not wanting to embarrass her in front of Dan.

Her slight grin tripped his heart. She reached into her pocket and pulled out a small notebook. In tiny, neat letters it said, "I'm fine. I'd like to sit outside."

So she knew he'd protest.

"If you're sure." He pulled her closer, wanting to shield her from hurt.

She patted his chest, letting her grin transform into a bright smile.

"Okay. I'll find you a seat."

"Before you get too comfortable, I have something I'd like to talk to you about." Dan strode across the camp, hefted up the wooden box Otto stored tools in, and plopped it with a thunk next to the still-empty fire pit.

"All right." Dread pooled in Otto's stomach as he led Klara to the box.

"Well, here's the thing. Robert Sweeney, a friend of mine, got himself married a few days ago and is taking his bride Sparrow back to see her family. He built a cabin down valley a bit. Long story short, I bought the place from him."

Klara tipped her head and scribbled on her pad. She lifted it to Otto.

"Won't they need it?" Otto read the question already on the tip of his tongue.

Dan crossed his arms and chuckled. "I told him I'd sell it back to him, but that boy's not coming back this way. I can guarantee it. You know love makes a man do some mighty peculiar things."

Dan winked at Klara. Otto gritted his teeth as his wife blushed prettily in the dress he'd bought her, even though there was a less expensive option. Yep. A man did peculiar things for a woman. Not that he was in love, but he didn't think it'd be hard for him to tumble down that slick slope.

"Well, congratulations on your new home. I'm surprised you're settling down." Otto bent to the firewood and snagged a piece to turn into kindling.

"I'm not settling quite yet." Dan stared off toward the west, his voice turning wistful. He shook his head and continued, "No, son, I'm heading up Crystal Creek to check on friends, and I'm late doing it. I don't plan on coming back this way until next summer."

"That's a shame. It would've been nice to have you as a neighbor this winter." Otto placed two hits on the wood's end and set the smaller section in the fire pit.

"That's what I'd like to talk to you about." Dan pulled on his scruffy red beard. "I don't want that cabin sitting empty all winter. Someone's liable to come by and jump the claim in my absence."

Otto swallowed the guilt and pain the mining phrase shot to his throat. He knew all about claim jumpers and wouldn't put it past any of the rabble hanging around Fryingpan Town to decide the cabin was theirs. He placed the hatchet down and tipped his head at Dan.

Dan nodded. "I knew you'd understand."

Understand what? Otto hated feeling two steps behind. He lifted his eyebrow while he attempted to relax his clenched jaw.

"Now, hear me out." Dan raised his hands in front of him in surrender. "This cabin of mine is solid, and just down yonder a mile or so up the creek. You'd be further from the riffraff at Fryingpan Town, and you'd have plenty of space to let the sheep graze."

"You want us to live in your place?"

Trapper Dan nodded.

"I don't know. I've already got the sheepfold set up. Moving would mean days of work making it safe for the flock." Otto shrugged off the tightening in his chest.

Dan had a legitimate need. He wasn't asking out of charity, but the sense of that still had Otto on edge.

"Sure, *you* would be comfortable enough, but it's not just you anymore." Dan tipped his head to Klara, jerking Otto's gaze to her.

He was so wrapped up in his hurt and pride that he forgot she was there. She sat with her arms crossed over her chest and a fiery look of challenge on her face. Had he ever seen anything more beautiful?

She motioned her hand to the tent, then mouthed, "Fine."

"Well, now ma'am, I know it's fine. Your husband has this camp set up right nice, but you'd be doing me a mighty big favor if you'd stay the winter in my place. Come next summer, you can put up a cabin of your own right here in this same spot. With it being so close to winter, I doubt anyone else will be coming to settle." Dan sure knew how to spin a yarn.

He also knew how to make it sound like he'd be the one getting the charity, not Otto and Klara. But Otto knew all about the weight of accepting charity from others. Each time a sheep took sick, the debt he owed Orlando for giving him a second chance at life threatened to buckle him. Could he handle the pressure of more?

"I don't know, Dan." Otto's shoulders slumped. "This place is perfect for the sheep."

"I understand. Just come over there with me and take a look." Dan flicked his gaze to Klara when Otto finally looked up. "Won't take but an hour of your time, I promise."

Otto's eyes darted to Klara, before turning to his hand squeezed around the hatchet handle. She sat perfectly still, just her fingers picked at her skirt. She may have vehemently shown their tent was fine, but wintering with nothing but canvas to block the cold would quickly have her regretting that defiance. He closed his eyes as he remembered how little there was of her when he grasped her waist and the bony arm that had pressed against his side.

Would she even survive the winter in a tent?

He couldn't bear the thought of her dying because of his pride. He couldn't live through that. Not again.

Otto sighed. "All right. Let's take a look at what you've got."

He smacked the hatchet into the center of the wood and stood. Klara gazed up at him, but the lack of expression on her face revealed nothing of her thoughts. Otto wrapped his hand around her elbow and helped her up.

"Do you think you can ride?" Otto whispered, rubbing his thumb along the inside of her arm.

She shivered, her breath catching with a part of her pink lips, then nodded. His tiny wife was made of grit. He gave her a small smile and turned to the tent. He'd swallow his pride and live in Dan's cabin if it meant he could make life a little easier for Klara.

CHAPTER 10

Klara leaned back against Otto's chest, letting the rolling gait of the horse ease her tension. Dan led several paces ahead of them through a stand of fluttering golden aspens. She held the duster Otto had draped over her shoulders closed in one hand and had the other resting on the strong arm securely wrapped around her waist. She breathed in and out, desperately wanting to brace herself for what they were about to see.

She could tell by the reluctant tone in Otto's voice that he didn't want to move to the cabin. He'd called it charity, and she supposed he was correct. Yet, Dan had said he didn't want just anyone squatting, and she knew that could just as easily happen, too. Wasn't that what the Müller's had done when they'd found the little house outside of town empty?

She shifted and cringed as the sharp pain shot across her middle. She'd been too nervous to check her bandage this morning. Her skin had to be an ugly black and blue if how much she hurt was any indication. She wiggled again, scolding herself for not taking the time to straighten the rolling bandage. It bunched uncomfortably under her dress.

"I knew it was too soon for you to be out." Otto groused. "I'm sorry, Klara. I should've thought more about your injuries. You shouldn't be riding a horse."

She patted his arm and turned her face so he could see her mouth. He was so near, his gray eyes piercing her with concern, she almost forgot why she'd turned. She licked her dry lips, and his gaze darted to them.

"It's okay," she mouthed and patted his arm again.

Otto shook his head. "No, it's not. I should've known the riding would be too hard on you. Should've told Dan now wasn't a good time for sightseeing."

Warmth started in her core and spread to her fingers and toes. If her husband kept up this caring attitude, she'd be hard-pressed not to get her heart tangled up in love. It'd be foolish, what with him marrying her because there wasn't any other choice. Maybe she wasn't as smart as she thought she was.

Her hands flew in front of her to communicate she was okay before remembering Otto didn't know the language she and her father had learned when she had lost her voice. She held up a finger to motion Otto to wait and dug her notebook from her pocket. When she was done scratching her message, she held it up to him. He read, his body relaxing against her.

"I'm glad Lemy's got a smooth gait, but the trip is still bothering you. I can tell every time you shift or flinch."

Otto met her gaze when he talked. She liked that she felt seen. For so many years, people either ignored her altogether or shifted uncomfortably when she tried to communicate. She penciled another note, her cheeks heating at the confession.

"Your bandages came loose?" Otto's neck blushed, and she was glad for the camaraderie in her embarrassment.

She nodded and turned back forward. He swallowed loudly next to her ear. She didn't want him to worry so much about her. She'd manage—better than she had been before, because of him. He cleared his throat.

"I could help you re-wrap your injuries." He cleared his throat again, and her blush rushed back, extending to her ears and hairline. "That is, you won't be able to wrap your ribs properly by yourself, and I don't mind giving you a hand with it."

Could she let him see all her bruises and jutting bones? Did she have a choice? She'd already been pondering how she'd get the bandage smooth so it didn't rub or bother her like it did now. Yet, letting herself be vulnerable—exposed—didn't sit right.

She closed her eyes and let the steady clop of the horse's hooves calm her. They were married now, and even though Otto said it'd just be in name only, a not so small part of her wanted it to be more. She didn't want a loveless marriage, and to get that, she'd have to trust her husband. If nothing else, having him help her with the bandages would show what kind of man he really was. If he took advantage of the situation, she'd know to keep her guard up.

Otto blew out a breath that danced along her neck. "I'm sorry if I offended. I promise, I meant no disrespect or nothing untoward. I just don't want you hurting."

She turned and smiled before mouthing, "I know. Thank you."

"You're welcome."

Her husband's eyes held so much sadness it nearly broke her heart. Maybe they had more in common than she originally thought. Maybe taking that step toward friends and a fulfilling marriage wouldn't be such a big one.

Dan whistled a sharp note to get their attention, yanking Klara's gaze away from Otto. She flinched, and he groaned behind her, making her smile. When she focused on what Dan was pointing at, she didn't stifle her gasp of surprise fast enough.

A quaint cabin sat close to a clear creek under a cluster of cottonwoods. Birds flitted from the trees to the bushes, filling the area with glorious song. A jumble of boulders beckoned her from beside the creek to sit and enjoy the scenery.

Her eyes dragged back to the cabin, surprised again by the craftsmanship. The logs for the walls stacked higher than the other cabins she'd seen in the area. With the added height of the tall pitch in the roof, Otto wouldn't have to duck like he did in the tent. Smoke twisted lazily from a stone chimney peeking out from the back of the cabin. The builder had even made wooden shingles instead of stacking sod on the roof.

What drew her eyes and made her heart skip with joy most was the red clay prevalent in the area that had been used as chinking between the logs. No wind would get through like it had at the Müller's barn. But more than that, the warm tone filled her with a sense of hope —permanence.

Klara swallowed her excitement at the homey settlement. She couldn't let her reaction guilt Otto into doing something else he didn't want to do. Marrying her was burden enough.

"Welcome to my humble abode." Dan shot them a smile as he spread his arms wide. "Do you see now why I need your help?"

"It's a mighty fine place." There was something in Otto's voice that made her want to turn and see his expression, but she worried he'd see the excitement shining in hers.

"That it is." Dan motioned toward the field behind the cabin. "Yonder would be the perfect spot for your sheep. They'd have plenty of grazing that would lead away from Fryingpan Town instead of toward." He leaned the other way in his saddle, making it creak. "The water should run most of the winter without freezing up, and let me tell you, it's about the sweetest you'll ever drink. There's a stack of firewood already stored behind the cabin in a lean-to that will get you through most of the winter and easy pickings just down the creek when you start to run short."

"Hmm," Otto answered.

Klara pressed her lips together. The more Dan talked, the more she thought of the swindlers who sold soap on the city corners back home. Everything he said was true, but if he didn't button up that booming mouth of his, Otto might turn tail and hoof it back to the tent.

"Why don't you two go inside and look around while I water the horses?" Dan swung from his saddle.

Otto slid from behind her. She straightened, instantly missing his heat. His mouth curved just a little as he reached up to lift her down. He eased his large, gentle hands into the duster he insisted she wear, gripping around her hips, and effortlessly lifted her down, keeping his gaze locked with hers. Her head spun, and when her feet touched the ground, she stumbled into him. His hands spread wide across her back to steady her.

"You okay?" His whispered question was gruff, and his brow furrowed.

She inhaled a deep breath and nodded as she exhaled.

"Let's go take a look so I can get you home to bed." His eyes widened and ears turned as red as pickled beets. "I mean ... that is ... Doc said you need to rest and gallivanting all over the countryside isn't resting."

She stifled her smile and turned to the cabin. Otto kept one arm around her back and snagged the other hand, leading her toward the door like an invalid. His hand trembled in hers, and she peeked up at him just in time to watch his Adam's apple bob the length of his throat. She leaned into him, determined even more to help this kindhearted man however she could.

Comforting heat hit her the moment she stepped through the door. Her gaze darted from one precious corner of the cabin to the next. A smooth shelf holding a mug, plate, and bowl hung above a small counter with a wash bin. A homemade table with two similarly made chairs was pushed up under the window covered in a pretty deer hide. The rock chimney she'd seen outside went from the split log floor up the back wall in a beautiful mosaic pattern around the opening of a large fireplace complete with a hook holding a cast iron pot. A large bed made from twisting peeled cedar filled the opposite corner from the table.

Her mouth hinged open in awe, and she snapped it shut as Otto entered behind her. While the space wasn't all that big, it called to her. She longed to spend the winter pulled up to the fireplace, reading. Wanted to trace the red chink lines of clay around the cabin with her eyes until she had them memorized. Her gaze darted back to the bed, and she jerked her eyes away as her cheeks heated. She wouldn't dwell on the desire rising to curl up against Otto there.

Suddenly, she wasn't worried so much about whether or not Otto would agree to stay at the cabin for the winter. She bit her bottom lip. No, she feared her heart would break when they had to leave at winter's end.

CHAPTER 11

OTTO STEPPED out of the cabin with the heavy decision leadening his legs. He didn't want to accept any more charity he didn't deserve, especially since there was a good chance he'd destroy this chance like everything else. Plus, a presence he couldn't name saturated the place, leaving him both desiring to find the respite promised there and itching to swoop up his wife and gallop away. The odd contradiction had him off balance.

He breathed in, hoping the crisp autumn air would clear his head. Instead, the sharp cold danced spots in front of his eyes. He shook his head, horrified that a simple cabin affected him so much.

"So, what d'ya think?" Dan asked from his seat on a jumble of boulders next to the creek.

"Nice place."

Otto made his way to Dan, keeping his gaze on the flowing water. He stopped next to the boulders and hooked his thumbs over his belt so he wouldn't fidget. As the creek babbled over rocks and rustled low-hanging branches, peace radiated from his chest, spreading steadily to his toes and fingers. That's what the presence was: quietness.

"You feel that?" Dan's whispered question jerked Otto's wide-eyed gaze to the mountain man. "That there is the Comforter, the peace of God. Lots of prayers have been poured over this ground and murmured into the breeze from this spot."

Dan patted the boulder and stared Otto down. Every time Otto was around the big man, he felt as if his soul was bare and easily read. He swallowed and shifted his eyes away. The sense of unworthiness settled even more into Otto's gut.

"Not sure if this place will work," he mumbled.

He turned his gaze south toward Mount Sopris, already tipped white with snow, the lie coating his tongue like he'd eaten a handful of bitter chokecherries. The sheep could dig through the snow to graze the buried grass all winter in the meadows spread out around the cabin. Shoot, even the cabin had everything a body could need. More than needed, with the tall walls and homey warm tones.

"When I was younger, my family lived up Green River way." Dan's quiet voice drew Otto's attention. "My parents settled in a quaint valley and set up a trading post for travelers and traders. Soon, other families built cabins close by. Not many, mind you, but enough that we could have ourselves a rousing church service around the store's stove."

Dan stared out across the water as he disappeared into the past. Otto had heard many stories around the campfire from the boisterous mountain man, but none had ever had the deep grief-filled heaviness this one did. Otto wasn't sure he wanted to hear the tale, but he held his breath, transfixed in anticipation.

"Then, we kids grew up, and Laura Smithton had sparked something hot and fierce in my chest." Dan rubbed his fist over his heart. "We wanted to get married, but our parents said we were too young. They were right, but being young and invincible, I convinced her to run away with me. I'd grown up in the wilderness, after all, and could handle anything the mountains threw at us."

Dan scoffed and closed his eyes, a tear tracking down his cheek into his rusty beard. "Winter settled fast and deep that year, much faster than I could build us a proper shelter. We were far away from family with just a tent and my ego to keep us safe. Laura starved to death, cradled in my arms. I would've too if my friend Joseph Thomas hadn't stumbled upon our place between storms. Wish he hadn't."

That last was whispered so quietly the wind almost took it away before it hit Otto's ears. Dan blinked and turned misty eyes to Otto. His own vision blurred, and he swallowed the sorrow clogging his throat.

"Don't make the same mistake I did." Dan nodded toward Klara where she rubbed Lemy's nose.

Otto hadn't heard her follow him out. She hadn't stifled her joy at the cabin quickly enough for him not to notice. Had he been so selfish that she felt the need to hide behind the mask of indifference?

"It doesn't matter how you two became bound together. She's more precious than gold, the most priceless treasure God put on this earth for you, Otto Lee.

Don't be a fool like me and sacrifice her safety for your pride."

Dan's words branded Otto with purpose and protectiveness. Klara glanced at him. The sun filtered through her blonde hair that had escaped her hasty braid, highlighting the sharp, bruised cheekbones on her already too-thin face. It wouldn't take much for her to starve or freeze with her not having any reserves on her bones. Her cheeks pinked before she ducked her head back toward the horse.

Otto cleared his throat and pushed down his pride. "Can you spare the day to help us move?"

CHAPTER 12

Later that afternoon, Klara held tin mugs against her chest and glanced around the cabin. Joy sang in her heart like the birds chirping outside the opened door. Happiness pulled her cheeks into a smile that warmed with a blush.

Oh, how her circumstances changed in such a short time. One moment she'd cowered under mildewy hay. The next she was safe within sturdy walls with a husband willing to sacrifice so much for her. She placed her hand on the side of her head, dizzy with emotion.

With a sigh, she set the two mugs on top of the shelf above the counter. Clapping her hands together, she scanned the room for anything she'd missed. After Dan had helped take down the tent, loaded Otto's camp into a small wagon the previous cabin's owner had left behind, and herded the sheep over the rolling meadows, Dan had taken off after a short prayer like his feet were on fire.

Otto had asked her to stay in the cabin and rest, but the excited energy rushing through her had made that impossible. So, she'd unpacked. Unfortunately, they had so few items between them that the task hadn't taken but thirty minutes.

She couldn't just lie about.

She needed to move, not wait within the isolating, silent walls. More than anything, she wanted the security the presence of her husband brought. She hated that fear lingered beneath her skin, but she couldn't shake it loose. Maybe she could help Otto with his tasks.

Stepping outside, she lifted her face to the warm fall sun. A breeze skittered through the dry grass and browning leaves, chilling her, but the sun banished the cold away like a gift just for her. Barking from behind the cabin jerked her from her silly notions. With a silent chuckle, she rounded the building and scanned the meadow.

A small, long-haired dog darted through the tall grass around the grazing sheep, chasing a ward that had wandered too far from the fold. She loved how the dog appeared to be smiling with his tongue hanging out the side of his mouth. It must say something about the character of her husband if his animals were so full of bliss.

Speaking of husbands, Klara shielded her eyes and scanned the meadow for Otto. Her gaze snagged on him, and she sucked in a shocked breath. He dragged a downed tree across the drying grass, his shirtless chest glistening in the sun. Her heart galloped beneath her ribs, threatening to pound right up her throat and out her mouth. She'd never seen a man in such undress before. Even if she had, she doubted they'd be as glorious as Otto.

She clutched her shawl in her fingers and willed her cheeks to cool as she ambled toward him. He tossed the tree into a pile, his arms bulging in the process. Klara willed the sun to go behind a cloud and the autumn breeze to kick up before she melted into the Colorado dirt. He turned away from her and stomped back to the grove of young cottonwood trees.

Sighing in relief, she swallowed to remove her heart from her throat, but the stubborn organ refused to dislodge. Then, as if to taunt her, Otto lifted an axe. Each *thwack* against the trunk flexed muscles across his back. Klara fanned her face as warmth built in her stomach and spread through her limbs. She should turn back before she fainted, consumed by this ache she couldn't name.

Her brow creased.

Embarrassment.

That had to be what she felt.

She shook her head. No, that didn't fit. Her intimacy with that emotion dismissed the suggestion immediately. She cocked her head to the side, and her eyebrows furrowed as she studied the warmth spreading like wildfire through her veins.

Otto glanced over his shoulder as he brought the axe back for another swing. His eyes widened when they caught sight of her staring, and the axe flew from his hands over his shoulder. It sailed through the air toward her. She slapped her hand over her mouth and jumped sideways out of the way. The head of the axe impaled the dirt with a *thump* where she'd stood.

"Klara!"

And there was her companion, embarrassment, scolding her for being caught staring.

Otto rushed to her, wrapping her arm with one hand and cupping her cheek with the other. Fear blasted from his eyes like a discordant trumpet blow. His palm shook against her cheek.

She placed her hand over his and pressed it to her face and mouthed, "I'm okay."

"Good Lord above, woman."

He dropped his hands with a shaky huff. She swayed with the sudden release. His hands found her waist, steadying her, and her palms pressed against the skin of his chest. His heart raced beneath her hand. She peered into his dark gray eyes full of concern. Her breath caught as understanding dawned bright as the morning sun over the Rockies.

The befuddling warmth spread desire to her soul. She wanted to know her husband and be known. She wanted to understand his thoughts and share his dreams. The need for her own dreams to be heard crescendoed loudly within her mind. Dreams of love and family and respect.

She flinched at the last, her fingers jerking against Otto's skin.

Hadn't she learned long ago that those dreams weren't ones she should put hope in?

No one had ever thought she'd do more than sit within the home and languidly play the piano—not even her parents, though they were more kind in their dismissal. She'd stopped challenging them, instead choosing to hide behind music that spoke her emotions for her, though no one heard the message.

"Steady now?" Otto asked, pulling her back to reality.

She nodded. He dropped his hands like she'd burned him and stepped out of her reach. Her fingers tingled with the residual sensation of his skin against hers. She gripped her hands into her skirt to hold on to the feeling just a little longer. His eyes darted to her fingers as a blush crept up his cheeks.

"Land sakes, Klara. You shouldn't sneak up on a man like that." He rushed to his shirt hanging from a branch and yanked it over his head so fast she was surprised he didn't rip the seams.

She rubbed her fist against her chest in the sign for sorry, then dropped it when she remembered he wouldn't understand.

"Why aren't you resting?" Otto stomped to the axe and hefted it from the dirt.

She opened her eyes wide and moved her hands next to her face, blinking her fingers open like eyelids.

He scrunched his forehead low. "You're wide awake?"

She nodded.

"But Doc said you should rest."

She barely suppressed the urge to roll her eyes and waved Otto off. Pulling out her notebook, she turned it so he could read the message already written there.

"You want to help me?" His head shook before he even finished reading. "You'll just get hurt more."

She scowled and uncovered the bottom half of the page that said she'd either help him there or work at the cabin. One of Otto's eyebrows rose. A dimple peeked from his cheek before disappearing with the pursing of his full lips. She jerked her gaze from them.

Otto ran his hand across his neck. "I don't know."

She pressed her palms together at her mouth in a begging motion. Emotion flashed in his eyes, but he banked it before she could read what it was. He pushed her hands down.

"Okay." He turned toward the tree, only to stop short.

"And Klara, you don't have to beg anything from me. You're not a prisoner. I don't own you. You're free to do as you please, even if what you want is to leave."

All this he said without looking at her, but it still expanded her heart with euphoria. She was a caged bird whose door had suddenly hinged open. She wanted to dance in the dirt. No, she wanted to pound her fingers across ivory keys until the joyful notes of her heart rang for all to hear.

When he turned his back fully to her, she heard him whisper, "I wouldn't blame you if you did."

The joy flipped and crashed to her feet. Why would she ever want to leave? He'd given her more in two days than she'd ever received in her entire life. While she pushed through the pain in her body and stacked small branches he hacked from the trees for her, the question circled in her head like a vulture. Never landing on an answer, but each rotation replaced warm excitement with confusion.

CHAPTER 13

Otto followed Klara as they made their way to the cabin. The sun hung close to the jagged mountains. Its fast descent darkened the eastern sky and stretched brilliant pinks and oranges from the west. He took a deep breath as he scanned the sky. Colorado sure knew how to paint a sunset.

Klara rolled her shoulders, drawing Otto's gaze to her. While he hadn't wanted her help, not with her still recovering, she'd cut his work significantly. What would've taken him at least three days to do on his own, she'd made it so they could have the sheepfold built by the next evening. He had watched her closely, only giving her light tasks and waiting for a sign she'd pushed too far, but it'd never come. All he'd witnessed was determination and soft smiles of satisfaction.

She stretched her neck, lifting one shoulder while pulling on the back of her dress. Dark purple bruising peeked from beneath the fabric. Otto's throat tightened.

In all the hustle of moving and chopping trees, he'd forgotten about her bandage needing rebound.

Of all the selfish, unthoughtful—

Otto clenched his teeth as he cursed himself. Here she'd spent the afternoon pushing herself to help him when she shouldn't have, and he hadn't had the brains to remember her simple need. He had to do better, *be* better. After what she'd been through with the Müllers, she deserved someone to put her first.

"Thank you for your helping me today." He lengthened his stride to catch up to her. The shocked, wide-eyed expression she turned to him twisted his heart and had him rushing on. "You really made the job easier, and I enjoyed having your company."

Her expression went from shocked to astonished confusion. Had no one ever complimented her? He knew the Müllers treated her worse than dirt, but had her own family? He smiled at her as he relaxed the fist he'd flexed.

She mouthed "company" and touched her throat. Her eyebrows scrunched low in question.

"Yes, your company. I like being around you."

He shrugged and turned his attention to the cabin, heat burning his ears. He peeked sideways at her as she bowed her head and touched her smile with her fingertips. His chest filled to bursting at putting the tilt of her mouth there.

"When we get to the cabin, I'd like to fix your bandages before we get supper." He snagged a leaf from the tall mountain grass and tossed it in front of him. "I'm sorry I forgot."

Her mouth dropped open and bruised cheeks blushed

before she snapped her lips closed. With a shake of her head, she mouthed, "I'm okay."

"Come on, Klara. You already agreed to let me help you." He raised an eyebrow in what he hoped came off as a jesting challenge. "Or do I have to worry about you going back on your word?"

Maybe that was the wrong phrase to say. He'd give her an out if she wanted. Shoot, he half expected her to take the first opportunity she got to head back home, wherever that was. He certainly would, knowing what he did about himself.

The thought of her leaving left an ache humming in his chest. He hadn't lied when he said he liked being around her. She was easy to be near. An enigma he wanted to solve but was also comfortable just being with. Her presence both confused him and eased the loneliness that had kept him company since his father's death. No ... since his sister and mother's deaths.

Klara huffed out a breath and glared at him. When she crossed her arms, she flinched in pain. Otto stopped and carefully smoothed his hand across her tight shoulders.

"I'm sorry. I didn't mean to offend." He dropped his hand, and she slowly lowered hers. "I know ... that is ... there's gonna be times we're uncomfortable with each other. Probably a lot."

He forced a laugh and rubbed the back of his neck. Could he possibly mess this up anymore?

Without a doubt he could.

Might as well just push through.

"But we're all we got, you and I. I hope that we can work through these uncomfortable situations to find even ground we're both agreeable to standing on."

She stared at him. Tears brightened her eyes, but she didn't look away. He wanted to keep talking, which would be pointless. Filling the space with empty words wouldn't get them anywhere. Finally, after a pause that felt like an eternity, she nodded. Her fingers moved in front of her belly as she mouthed, "Okay."

Relief rushed through him like a cool summer wind, and he heaved out a breath. "Okay, then. Let's get your bandages fixed so we can eat." He stepped toward the cabin, determined to make this task as easy as possible. "I don't know about you, but I'm starving."

Her fingers fumbled with her collar as she nodded. When they stepped into the cabin, he stopped short. His two extra shirts and pair of pants hung next to her other dress on nails she'd hammered into the wall at the base of the bed. A pantry of sorts with all the food he'd stored in the trunk lined the shelf above the counter where the few plates and cups rested. The storage trunk he'd unceremoniously dumped in the center of the space was pushed against the foot of the bed. Not only had she come and helped with his job, but she'd settled everything in place in the cabin as well.

"Looks right homey in here." He nodded at the space.

She smiled broadly up at him, making warmth spread to his fingers.

"Are the medical supplies still in the trunk?"

She bit her bottom lip and nodded, a soft pink rushing up her cheeks. He cleared his throat, then tipped his head toward the door while lifting his dirty hands up in front of him.

"I'll just go wash up in the creek real quick while you ... um—"

He stopped short. The only word that sprung into his head was "strip" and that seemed highly inappropriate. He swallowed, and when that didn't dislodge the ball of uncertainty in his throat, he cleared it again. His face scorched from his chin to his hairline.

Shoot.

He might have to dunk all the way into the freezing creek just to cool his embarrassment.

As he rushed out the door, he mumbled, "While you do whatever you need to do."

CHAPTER 14

A QUICK SNIFF under Otto's arm had proven he did need a good dunk for more than just cooling off. So, fifteen minutes later he stood, skin still chilled from his bath, with his knuckles rapping on the cabin door.

Only after the tapping sounded, did he remember Klara couldn't tell him to come in. He shifted from one foot to another. He didn't want to just barge in if she wasn't ready. What if she was still undressing? His heating skin evaporated the last of the water clinging to him, and he worried he'd have to take another swim.

A whistle from inside filtered through the door. He smiled at how similar it was to the one he used to get the sheep to follow him. Klara must've remembered it from that morning. Taking the notes as his sign to come to her, he slowly opened the door.

"If I mistook your whistle's meaning, just toss something at me, and I'll leave." Otto averted his eyes toward the cups on the shelf just in case.

A soft exhale, almost like a laugh, pulled his gaze to the

bed. She sat on the edge, with the top of her dress unbuttoned and folded over her hips and his rough wool blanket clutched to her front to cover her. Her bright blue eyes were wide on her face, but she gave him a trembling, small smile of encouragement.

"Ready?" His voice croaked in his throat like a frog.

She shifted but nodded, tipping her head at the bandage on the quilt.

"Right. Okay."

Otto clapped his hands and stomped over to the bed. No need to make a mountain out of a molehill. He'd helped his ma wrap bandages before. Sure, it wasn't on a beautiful woman—his wife, no less—but there wasn't any need for him to make things worse by being uneasy.

As he drew closer, she shifted the blanket with a trembling hand to just cover her front and turned away from him. Dark purple and red punched and slashed across ivory skin. Ribs marched down her sides, intersecting at her jutting backbone with little meat to hide any of them. A step closer and his gaze shifted to lighter green wrapping up around the skin of her shoulder.

She'd been abused prior to the day before.

Rage he'd never felt rushed like a wildfire through his veins. His hands pulsed with the need to hurt those who could do something so heinous to someone so innocent. His anger wouldn't help Klara in that moment, though, no matter how justified. He shook out his hands and unclenched his jaw.

"Oh, Klara."

He closed the few feet to the bed and sat behind her. He ran the back of his fingers across the top of her shoulder where the bruises were less. She shuddered, curling in on herself slightly, and he yanked his fingers away. She probably didn't want anyone touching her, maybe never again.

And he'd been hoisting her up and down off the horse, then working her pert near to death hauling trees. He *knew* he should've followed the doc's orders and made her stay in bed.

She looked over her shoulder and raised her eyebrows at him.

"Sorry. I shouldn't have let you work today."

Her questioning expression turned to a glare as she mouthed, "Let me?"

"Isn't it my responsibility to protect you, even if that's from yourself?" He motioned to her back, upset that his breath trembled when he blew it out. "This … this is just so much. Hauling wood and riding Lemy had to hurt you more."

Her glare softened. She squeezed his hand before pulling the bandage closer. The motion caused her to flinch in pain. Weariness darkened the skin below her eyes. He wished there was more he could do to help than just wrap her back up.

"Hold on." He stood and rushed to the trunk at the foot of the bed. "I have something that might help with the pain."

He dug through his belongings, pushing things left and right. Finally, his hand grazed over the cool tin canister he searched for. He pulled it out with a grimace.

"Now, I know this liniment is for horses, but I've used it a few times when I've hurt myself and it helps."

She nodded and turned back around. He blew out a nervous breath, rubbed a small amount between his fingertips to warm the ointment up, then, as gently as he could, smeared it on her skin. He started on the lightest bruises, because if his touch proved too much, he didn't want to make the dark, almost black bruises worse.

"Let me know if I'm hurting you," he whispered.

She nodded, taking a short breath in and holding it. He dipped his fingertip into the canister and repeated the process over and over again until all her back glistened with the medicine and her muscles had relaxed. He trailed his fingers around her waist, following the bruises wrapping toward her belly.

"Your front is hurt, too." He didn't ask. It was clear as day, but she nodded in answer. "Let's get some medicine there as well."

She swallowed and bundled the blanket higher on her chest. He kneeled in front of her to get a better angle, but the bulk of the wool obscured his view of her skin. He scowled in frustration and rocked back on his heels, his eyes scanning the cabin for anything that could help. They snagged on his shirt hanging on the peg, and he rushed to it.

"Here. Put this on." He shoved it at Klara and turned around to give her privacy. "There's less fabric there to deal with."

Rustling filled the quiet, and he shifted on his feet. She whistled a note that rose. When he turned, the vulnerability in her eyes had him clearing his throat. It was one thing to glide his fingers over her back. It was a whole other thing for her front, even if it was just her belly.

"Better?" Otto asked.

She nodded, then lay back on the mattress, her arm draped over her to hold his shirt to her chest. He groaned as he took in the bruising marring her skin. Somehow, he'd hoped it wouldn't be so bad.

"I'm so sorry, sugar." He clenched his jaw and gently started the process over. "You should never have had this happen."

Tears formed in her eyes, and her lips drew his gaze. "Thank you."

"One of these days, when you feel better, you'll have to tell me how you ended up with those varmints." He went back to his ministrations. "They claimed to be family, but that's a lie. So, how'd you end up there? Don't you have any family?"

A tear traced down her cheek. She shook her head and turned her face to the side. He didn't blame her. What an insensitive mule he was rattling on like that.

"Forget I asked."

He went back to his job in silence. Only the occasional sniff from Klara and clink of the metal tin filled the air. Eventually, the tension eased, replaced by a sense of relaxation, and he almost hated that he'd come to the end of bruises and had her bandaged up.

"Done." He rubbed his palms together, then capped the tin. "Why don't you take your dress the rest of the way off and scootch into bed. With how small you are, my shirt will cover to your knees and will be more comfortable than your dress to sleep in. I'll get dinner going while you rest."

He turned his back to her and dropped the ointment back into the trunk.

"I should have thought about getting you a nightdress. We'll pick one up next time we go to town or, if you know how to sew, we can purchase some fabric." And there he went rambling like the village fool again.

The movement of the bedding stopped. She'd curled up on her side against the wall facing toward the rest of the room. She looked so small and delicate, not someone who could handle the rigors of the West.

Doubt plopped in his gut like a heavy rock tossed into a clear pond. The force rippled through the rest of his body. What if he couldn't keep her safe? What if he screwed up again and she ended up like Dan's wife, dead because of Otto?

He watched as her throat bobbed with a swallow before she patted the bed beside her. He wrinkled his forehead in confusion but sat down anyway. She mouthed "thank you," and he shook his head instantly.

"I haven't done much."

Oh, he'd done so much worse than that. He'd shackled her to a selfish coward.

"I'll go rustle us up something to eat." He went to move before she saw the truth of him.

Her hand clamped over his, stopping him.

"Stay." She mouthed and patted his side of the bed.

"You want me to stay?"

It wasn't like he was going far. The cabin wasn't all that big. She nodded, so he lay down facing her.

She gave him a small smile, then her lips moved. "Safe."

"Safe?" He couldn't have read her word right.

Yet, she nodded.

"I make you feel safe?" He asked incredulously.

Her nod was small, like the confession embarrassed her. It made him feel like Hercules. He took a deep breath, letting the feeling soak in a bit.

"Okay. I'll stay."

She didn't move any closer, and neither did he. Her gaze studied him for several minutes while he tried not to fidget. Finally, her eyelids drooped, and after several blinks, they fluttered closed.

He watched her as the last of the tension left her body. Watched her as the fire she'd built while she waited for him to wash up burned low and only embers lit her bruised cheeks. Eventually, his lids grew weighted. Only then, when exhaustion forced its heaviness upon him, did he close his eyes and sleep.

CHAPTER 15

Klara refused to cry over bacon so charred she could write songs with it if she had paper. There was still hope that the biscuits would be edible. She dubiously eyed the cast iron hanging in the fireplace. Thin hope, but it still existed.

She wished she could blame it on cooking over an open fire, but she couldn't. Here she was a grown woman of nineteen, and thanks to her affluent upbringing, she'd never been taught to cook. She couldn't speak, her bruises and pain kept her from truly helping her husband, and she cooked like Elijah on Mount Carmel.

Surely no man could put up with so many downsides, would he? Her nose stung, and she fluttered her eyelashes to dry the useless tears. After waking up to an empty house and spying Otto already in the field, she'd wanted to make breakfast for him. What she'd made was a mess, wasting precious food in the process.

When Otto walked in and received burnt offerings, she wouldn't cry when he annulled the marriage. She understood, had been prepped growing up that no man would ever want her. The only way she got a husband in the first place was because Trapper Dan pressured poor Otto. Her husband was just too kindhearted to see what a hopeless case he was agreeing to take on.

Maybe she should just leave on her own accord. She'd seen the tiny log church on their way out of town. If she appealed to the pastor, maybe he'd allow her to stay there until passage could be secured for Ohio. Pulling her weight wasn't a problem, when she wasn't injured, and she didn't mind cleaning and gardening, though her mother would be appalled.

Klara scrubbed her palms over her face in despair. The thought of leaving tore at her heart. She felt safe with Otto. His tender care of her bruises the night before hadn't just calmed the soreness but had soothed her soul. She couldn't remember the last time anyone had done that. She'd been nine when she'd lost her voice. Her father had never allowed wallowing in hurts, so any hurts she received got her a pat on the shoulder and encouragement to buck up. After the bee attack, her mother hadn't known how to deal with a child that wasn't whole. So slowly, she pulled away from Klara.

The smell of overdone bread hit her nose, jerking her out of her sulking. With a gasp, she rushed to the fireplace and swiveled the hook holding the pan away from the flames. Half of the biscuits appeared overdone. They weren't burnt like the bacon, but their coloring was the shade of rich mud. She poked her finger into the other half. Soft, sticky dough met her touch.

How was that even possible?

Huffing, she crossed her arms and glanced into the

flames. No use staring at the problem. Maybe if she watched the pan extra close, she could save the other half from being bricks. Wrapping her apron around the handle, she grunted against the pain in her back and stomach lifting the pan caused. She hung the pan back on the hook so the unbaked biscuits would cook and swiveled the food over the fire.

Rushing to the counter, she pulled the plates and forks from the shelf. She had at least a few minutes to set the table and wipe the last of her mess up before her vigilance would be required. A sharp pain spiked through her back as her muscles spasmed, making her knees weak. She barely kept from collapsing completely by bracing herself with the counter edge. Sweat broke out across her forehead. She closed her eyes and breathed through the pain.

The soft scrape of the door registered the instant before Otto's worried voice filled the cabin. "Klara!"

Of course he'd come home now. Life never gave her any breaks. Expecting them would just be naïve.

"Klara, sugar, what's wrong?"

She sure did like the sound of that nickname rolling off his tongue. It filled her with warmth and giddiness like when her family's cook would give her a gooey cinnamon roll still warm from the oven as a child. What she didn't like was that he only said it in pity.

In answer, she shook her head and raised her hand in dismissal.

"I meant to get back earlier to put some more liniment on you, but time got carried away from me." He cupped the back of her head, rubbing his thumb down the center of her neck.

His tenderness comforted her, allowing her shoulders

to relax. She took another deep breath as the spasm eased and turned so her back rested against the counter. Otto's forehead furrowed in worry as he gazed at her.

She patted him on the chest and mouthed, "I'm fine."

"You sure?" He stepped closer as his hand trailed down her arm, then pinned her hand to his chest.

She swallowed and nodded. His eyes bounced from one side of her face to the other like he searched for whether she told the truth or not. He leaned closer, his palm pressing more firmly to her hand. His heart pounded against her skin, picking up pace.

She couldn't breathe.

Couldn't move.

His gaze dipped to her suddenly parched lips. She licked them and tried to swallow, but her mouth and throat were just as dry. The desire to be kissed by this man evaporated every other thought in her head. Mere inches separated them, but it felt like miles. Was she brave enough to close the distance?

He sniffed and wrinkled his nose. Oh, dear Lord above. Did she still stink like horse liniment and sweat? She'd tried to clean up but couldn't reach everywhere.

She took a breath through her nose, and the smell of burnt bread hit her. She gasped, pushed past Otto, and rushed to the fire. How had the biscuits burned so quickly? She reached for the hook, but a large hand settled on her hip while the other wrapped around her hand stretching carelessly for the hot metal.

"Here. Let me." Otto's low voice tumbled over her.

She glanced up into his gray eyes. They sparkled with humor, but she didn't see anything funny about burning breakfast. He eased her to the side and pulled the pan from the fire.

"My ma always joked with Pa about distracting a cook in the kitchen. Said it was the quickest road to overdone food." Otto turned from the fire and gave Klara a wink. "Pa always said the distraction was worth it, and I'm thinking he had it right."

Her neck and ears heated as she darted to the counter to place the trivet she'd found. Little did Otto know that she didn't need a husband's diversion to char the meal. Would he still wink and joke when he noticed the charcoal bacon?

She backed against the cabin wall as he placed the pan down. His eyes snagged on the plate of bacon, his eyebrows winging up. He coughed, then glanced at her in question.

She clenched her fist and rubbed her fingers against her chest in a circle in the sign for "sorry." Like the simple word released all the others bound up since her parents' deaths, her hands flew in front of her as words tumbled forth.

"I'm so sorry. I can't cook. Everything burns. If not, it probably wouldn't be edible." Her chest heaved as she continued, her hands racing through the words. "No one taught me. No one taught me anything of use."

"Hey." Otto swept her hands into one of his, trapped them against his chest, and cupped her cheek with the other. "Slow down, sugar."

She took a giant breath, begging her heart and words into control. Her hand twitched within his, and he ran his thumb along the length of the back of her fingers. His eyes were wide in shock, and she closed hers so she wouldn't see the shock morph into disdain like most people.

"Sorry," she mouthed.

"Klara, what were you doing with your hands?" He removed his palm from her cheek and lifted both of her hands in his before dropping them.

With her back pressed against the cabin wall, she dug into her pocket for the pad and pencil. "Sign language."

His eyebrows winged up toward his hairline. "Like the Indians?"

The language she used had originally come from France when Laurent Clerc brought it to America, but it wouldn't matter. She pressed her lips together and gave a curt nod, bracing for the words she'd heard from others for so many years. *Vulgar. Primitive. Ugly.* Each whispered but heard all the same. People assumed since her voice didn't work, her ears didn't either.

"That's brilliant."

The wonder in Otto's voice jolted her. He snatched her hand not holding the pencil and paper, twisting it this way and that as he examined them. She held her breath, not knowing if she could trust his awe.

"It was so breathtaking, like your hands danced in front of you." He threaded his fingers with hers, then met her gaze. "I want to learn. I want to know what's in that beautiful head of yours. Can you teach me?"

Her mouth dropped open, and her heart filled with so much joy she worried it'd spew from her gaping maw. He wanted to learn her language? Her own mother hadn't wanted to learn. More importantly, he thought her head was beautiful?

"Yes," she mouthed, then she slid the paper and pencil

in her pocket, and, with her free hand, she made a fist and rocked it forward like a head nodding while mouthing "yes."

"Yes." He repeated the motion with his own fist, a smile blooming across his face. "This is great. At night, after chores, you'll teach me. During the day, don't hold back. Let the words flow. Maybe I can pick up a few here and there just by seeing you use them."

She must be dreaming. At any moment, she would wake up and find herself back in the musty hay stacked in the Müller's barn. Life wouldn't allow her to have the perfect man as a husband, not with how harsh it had been to her so far.

He stepped back, his gaze landing on the charred breakfast with a grimace. Now, the disgust would come. She dropped her hands to her sides and pushed them against the log wall.

"Don't worry about breakfast. I have some jerky we can eat for now." Otto tipped his head toward the fireplace. "Cooking over the flame like that's difficult. You teach me words. I'll teach you how to use our fireplace."

He winked at her, opened the door, and strode outside. Thank goodness she leaned against the solid wall behind her, because she wasn't sure her legs would hold. The autumn air whipped in like a slap in the face. She pushed off the wall and squared her shoulders.

Her husband seemed the understanding sort. None of her deficiencies appeared to bother him. When he showed her how to cook in the fireplace, she'd just swallow her pride and ask him to teach her how to cook as well. If she could learn the basics, with practice, she was sure she could figure out the rest.

CHAPTER 16

Klara checked the stew she'd set over the fire several hours before. The thick brown gravy bubbled and glistened around the chunks of mule deer, potatoes, onions, and carrots. She'd figured something full of liquid would be safer against burning, especially since she'd kept the fire low and stirred the pot often, making sure to scrape the bottom.

The test bite she'd taken had proved her theory right. It wasn't the best tasting bite she'd ever had, but it wasn't burnt. Hopefully, Otto liked stew because they'd be eating a lot of it. Kind of like the Israelites in the desert surviving on only manna and quail. She'd just have to keep practicing other meals alongside the stew so Otto wouldn't end up grumbling about eating the same thing morning, noon, and night.

She glanced around the room and sat with a sigh on the chair at the table. Otto had begged her to rest instead of helping him, claiming they'd tackled the hard work the day before. Everything in her had wanted to go against him, to prove her worth, but she'd relented. In truth, she'd been so sore and exhausted that resting throughout the day had been a healing blessing. She'd taken time to scrub her charred mess from the pot, slowly cut up the ingredients for the stew, making sure to have all the pieces even, then, after it hung to cook, took a nap. When she'd woken with a start, hurrying to check the stew, and found the mixture still intact, she'd cleaned up the already clean cabin.

Now, as she waited for Otto to arrive home, she painstakingly drew hand diagrams of words they'd most often use in her notebook. She had to be careful and not make mistakes. There weren't very many blank pages left, but it would give them a start. Her plan was to work through part of the alphabet and a few words each night if her husband still wanted to learn after he'd had time to think it through.

Steps sounded on the other side of the fur-lined window opening. Her calm of the day instantly vanished to heart-pounding anticipation. She stood, her gaze darting around the room for something to do so she didn't look lazy. To her dismay, everything was already in order and set for dinner. The door opened a crack, snapping her attention to it.

"Knock, knock, wife."

Otto's friendly tone sounded more tired than normal. She knew she should've helped him instead of lounging around the cabin all day. She swallowed down the guilt and whistled his tune for come. His smile as he opened the door fully washed most of the guilt away.

"You sure do know how to whistle a pretty tune." He took a deep breath, and his eyes widened in surprise as his stomach rumbled. "Whatever you have cooking smells delicious."

She pressed her lips together to keep from smiling like a silly child. Hurrying to the fire, she wrapped her apron around the metal hook and rotated it out of the fire. A warm hand settled on her hip a second before the heat of Otto's body radiated behind her.

"Here, let me." His words rumbled along her neck, tangled in the tiny hairs there, and sent a shiver of delight down her spine.

She stepped back, but he didn't move. He stared at her, his gaze dipping to her lips and back up.

"Thanks for making supper." His voice lowered, coming out gravelly.

She bit her lip and nodded. His eyes followed the action as his body leaned closer. This was it. Her handsome husband was finally going to kiss her. Seconds stretched into ages as the space between them lessened millimeter by millimeter. A sharp bark jerked him away.

Otto chuckled, his neck reddening as he glanced at the dog sitting by the door. "Right. Supper time."

He dropped his hand from Klara's hip, and she instantly missed the heat of it. She stepped away, glaring at the interrupting creature, and attempted not to stomp out her frustration as she crossed to the counter where the trivet sat waiting for the pot. Why couldn't he just forget everything around them and kiss her, for goodness' sake? She certainly had. Shoot, lightning could've struck at her feet, and she'd have sworn it was the electricity stretching between her and her husband.

As Otto brought the steaming pot over, she leaned against the counter and stared down at their chaperone.

She remembered this one, much smaller than the other, darting tirelessly through and around the flock the day before as it made sure all the sheep stayed close. The other dog, white and as large as a bear, had simply lounged about, its head twisting every now and then to take in the scenery.

"I got the sheepfold done enough that Duke here doesn't need to stay out at night anymore." Otto set the pot down, then mirrored her lean against the counter. "I hope you don't mind, but Duke usually sleeps with me. Baron, the big, white Pyrenees, guards better without this guy pacing all night."

"OK," she mouthed and signed the letters.

Otto mimicked her fingers, smiling as he said, "OK." He turned to the pot and grabbed a bowl waiting on the counter. "Why don't you have a seat, and I'll serve this up?"

Klara was halfway to the table before she realized she should have served him. She didn't want him always coddling her. She wanted to be his helpmate, equally sharing the burden of jobs. Sure, he'd always be able to do more than she could simply because of his massive size and strength, but she didn't want him doing the jobs she could easily do, as well.

With determination to do better firmly in her mind, she sat at the table and watched Otto scoop out the stew she prayed was edible. He'd rolled up his sleeves at some point in the day. His muscles flexed, and veins bulged and twisted down his arm with each motion. How could something as mundane as a forearm make her insides heat and her mouth go dry? Maybe letting her husband help with her chores wasn't such a bad idea after all.

Duke's claws clicked along the wood floor, jerking her attention from ogling her husband. She sucked in a breath, her hand going to her throat. The dog only had three legs.

"What's wrong? Are you hurting?" Otto quickened his stride, placing the filled bowls on the table before setting his hand on her shoulder.

She shook her head and pointed at the dog. Then she held up three fingers, then moved her hands like legs walking. Otto's concern wrinkling his forehead smoothed, and he sat across from her.

"Yep. Duke only has three legs. Wouldn't know it from the way he races through the sheep, would you?" He picked up his spoon and looked at her shaking her head in response. "A few months after I got him, he got stuck in a wolf trap. I had to amputate his leg and stitch him up. Those next four months were some of the worst I've ever had. I almost lost him several times, but he kept pulling through."

Why in the world would someone go through so much trouble for a dog? She searched for how to ask without offending. Her confusion must have shown.

"What? You can ask me anything, Klara. You don't have to mince words with me." Otto set his spoon in his bowl and leaned his elbows on the table in an easy manner.

Not wanting to take the time to write, she signed the easiest thing she could think of. Making a gun out of her fingers, she pretended to shoot Duke, then lifted both hands up in question.

"Why didn't I just shoot him?" Otto asked, his tone making sure he understood. When she nodded, he continued, "I couldn't. Duke is just about the only friend I have, my best friend, really, and if I could save him, I was going to do my best to try. Besides, just because Duke lost a bit of himself doesn't mean he lost his usefulness and excitement for life. Once he healed up, it wasn't long before he figured out how to use the legs he had left and was off chasing sheep again."

That warmth that had smoldered in her gut a few minutes earlier burst into flames and filled her with so much hope that she thought she might combust. She tore her stare from Otto and studied the dog, having no problem sitting on his haunches and batting a front paw in a beg. Where most people would see a dead dog, her husband not only showed love and caring, but the potential still left to one so broken. If he saw that in an animal, surely he could see a future for her that was more than just staying stuck inside behind the piano or book.

Could God have brought her out here to this wilderness to meet the only man who could see her worth? It seemed an extreme thing to do, but the truth remained. Her sudden husband was perfect for her, but she didn't want the relationship to be one-sided.

All she needed was time to heal. While she did, she'd help in whatever ways she could. The kindhearted and caring person she found herself married to deserved someone to come alongside him and help, proving she still was useful and had excitement for life, too.

CHAPTER 17

Otto glanced across the meadow, his gaze skimming over bleating balls of wool until it landed on Klara on the opposite side. When he'd said he was going to take the sheep north to graze away from the homestead for the day, she'd insisted on coming along. It was too soon. She should be resting like the doc said, but Otto couldn't deny her anything when her expressive blue eyes looked up at him with such hope.

A jaunty tune whistled in the air, accentuated with sheep bleats. Twin lambs trailed behind Klara like the nursery song, "Mary Had a Little Lamb." They occasionally butted their noses against Klara's hand until she scratched behind their ears. Many sheep had taken to coming up to her throughout the morning, which was unlike them. It made sense, though. Her sweet spirit was like a magnet, drawing beast and man to her.

Otto shifted in the saddle, tearing his gaze from her to make sure the sheep he'd found wandering off hadn't slipped away again. He'd set Duke to stay close to Klara for protection, so Otto had to be extra vigilant on this first scavenge from home. He needed to keep the sheep grazing as far from the homestead as possible during the day. They'd need the meadows close to the cabin for winter.

A sharp breeze lifted his kerchief tied around his neck and raised goose bumps across his skin. He scanned the mountains again, not liking how the white snow tips had spread further down overnight. Winter wasn't far off, and he wasn't prepared.

How was he possibly going to keep the sheep alive through the winter? He had no way of baling hay yet. They'd made it through the last winter, but it had been a mild one with little snow. What if the coming cold brought several feet of the white stuff? Would the Roaring Fork valley that was perfect for ranching in the summer fill up too deep to graze during the winter?

This was why he never should have accepted the sheep in the first place. He didn't know enough about shepherding. When the animals perished from his ill planning, his friend Orlando would lose precious resources, and Otto would be left without a way to support his family.

His eyes winged back to Klara. He probably shouldn't have married her, either. He'd failed at protecting his dad. He'd brought sickness home to his family, killing his mother and sister. Everywhere he went death and heartache followed.

Klara tilted her head back, lifting her face to the sun. He could see her smile and peace even all the way across the meadow. This woman who'd been through so much didn't deserve more pain that would come if he wasn't able to provide for her.

He pressed his hand over his heart to hold in the fear pounding there. It didn't matter what his past was. The curses of his past didn't have to follow into his future. Wasn't that what the Bible said? He could move forward in confidence and strength, knowing God would provide their needs as long as Otto was faithful to do his part.

He *would* move forward in that.

Anything less would leave room for failure and attack.

Klara's whistle cut off mid-note. He blinked to focus from his woolgathering, narrowing his eyes on her. She rubbed her side, her face pinched in pain. Though she wouldn't admit it, she needed a break. Well, there were more ways to help his wife than being direct. He smiled at how he already knew she'd push herself too hard and urged Lemy through the flock.

When she saw him coming, she jerked her hand from her side, smiled broadly and much too fake, and waved. He shook his head at her as she tried to hide her pain. He'd have to remember that in the future and watch for cues to how she really felt. Not that he minded one bit keeping a close eye on his pretty wife.

"I think this is as good a spot as any to let the sheep graze." He motioned Duke to keep the sheep close and swung down from the saddle. "Where do you think would be better to sit for a spell, the spot under the tree?" He pointed to a large cottonwood whose branches stretched wide for shade. "Or the rocks?"

Her gaze followed his finger to the patch of grass alongside a jumble of boulders. Lips tweaking to the side in consideration, her eyes bounced from one place to the other. She set her elbow on the back of one hand and pointed her forearm up, waving her fingers like leaves blowing in the breeze.

"Tree?" He copied her sign.

She nodded and beamed at him.

"Good pick."

He grabbed Lemy's reins so he wouldn't give into the temptation to hold her hand and headed toward the tree. When they got close, he dropped the reins to the grass to ground hitch Lemy, then dug in the saddlebags. Otto pulled out the wool blanket he'd snagged from his trunk and handed it to Klara. Next, he dug out the jerky and two of the wild plums he'd found the day before.

Her excitement when he'd told her about the tree he'd discovered along the creek and showed her the dark, purple fruits had made him want to scour the area for more treasures to bring her. They'd have to dry as many plums as they could for winter. The store in Fryingpan Town might have canning supplies, but he doubted either of them knew how to preserve the fruit properly.

He followed her under the branches, set their lunch on a rock so a woolly thief didn't steal it, and helped her spread the blanket out on the grass. Her contented release of breath after she sat told him his ploy to get her to rest couldn't have come at a more perfect time. After gathering the food, he settled beside her, his shoulder rubbing against hers.

Perfect.

Choosing the smaller of his two blankets worked out just like he planned. Because of the limited space, he could sit close to his wife without raising her suspicions. He stretched out his legs and leaned back a little, bracing himself with his hands. He barely suppressed his smile now that his arm stretching behind her back almost felt like an embrace. It reminded him of being at barn dances back in Kansas when he was sparking different girls, back when life was carefree.

Klara turned her head to him, her chin tucked shyly. As her cheeks pinked, she lifted her gaze to meet his. Hope and longing galloped in his chest like a herd of wild mustangs.

"You're a natural shepherdess." His voice came out all gravelly, so he cleared his throat.

She shrugged off his comment and picked at her skirt. Why did she not believe in her ability? He wanted to capture her gaze again.

"I think you're better than me." That got her head snapping up and shaking. He chuckled. "Seriously, it took me weeks to get them to trust me. One morning with you, and I think they'd follow you to the moon."

She rolled her eyes and swatted his chest. Quick as a rattler, he caught her hand in his and leaned closer.

"Thank you for coming along with me today." Keeping from staring at her lips when they were this close was a Herculean feat. "It's much nicer knowing someone else is here with me. Your sweet tune carrying on the wind makes me feel not so alone."

Her stare darted back and forth, bouncing from one of his eyes to the next, like she searched for the truth of his words. Those galloping mustangs escalated to a full-out stampede. Her pulse on her wrist captured beneath his fingertips raced just as fast.

Their marriage may have been one of convenience, but his bumbling words at their wedding about the marriage just being for her protection was a blaring inconvenience. More than anything, he wanted to wrap her in his arms and kiss her until they were both breathless. Those hasty words he'd spewed in front of the doctor's tent kept him firmly where he was.

She opened her mouth, giving him reason to look. He very well couldn't read her lips if he wasn't watching them. She slammed them shut, pressing them tightly together with a huff of frustration and turning her head away.

He rubbed his fingertip along her wrist and whispered, "What is it, sugar?"

She jerked her attention back on him, her stare steady as she took a deep breath. Quickly, she leaned forward and brushed her lips to his. It was over much too fast for his liking.

When she pulled back, her cheeks bright pink with blush, she mouthed, "Thank you."

He pressed her hand still held in his against his chest, then he ran his other hand up her spine, skimming along her neck until he cupped the back of her head. He gently pressed his lips to one side of her mouth.

"Thank *you*, Klara." He moved to the other side of her mouth and kissed there. "Thank you for giving me life again…purpose."

She sucked in a breath, tensing, and he captured her surprise with his lips. Her release of tension as she leaned into him soared him higher than one of those fancy hot air balloons. Her touch was tentative as she kissed him back, so he reined in his desire for more of her.

He kissed her cheek, then her forehead. She sighed and tucked her head against his chest. Wrapping his arms gently around her, he couldn't help but believe in the promise of a future marrying Klara gave him. Winter may be fast approaching, but hope bloomed through his veins like a mountain meadow in summer.

CHAPTER 18

Klara smiled into the pot of stew as she danced a little jig while she stirred. The last week had been the most glorious days of her life. More rewarding than the time she'd performed at the neighborhood talent show and surprised all the attendants with her music. More splendid than her family's trip to Paris and all the museums and concerts they took in. Even more exhilarating than the three-ring circus that had left her dreaming for days of running away from her stifling life to swing among the stars.

Each day she and Otto had explored the area while the sheep grazed. He'd shown her the wild plum tree and talked of planting seeds and starting an orchard. Her heart had plinked a jaunty beat with those words. It would take years for fruit trees to mature—years her husband planned on being with her.

She tapped the large wooden spoon on the side of the pan and twirled away from the fireplace. Her whistled tune picked up as more memories of the last few days sprang to mind. His eager study of the sign language only her father had taken the time to learn. The looks of admiration she'd catch Otto giving her way. The tender kisses stopped much too soon for her liking.

That last thought brought heat to her cheeks as she closed her eyes, tipped her head back, whistled through the bagatelle at an extra fast pace, and twirled in the center of her homey cabin. This life proved better than any she'd ever imagined.

A low chuckle whipped her around, her whistle ending in a shocked, shrieking sound. Otto leaned on the doorjamb, an amused grin on his face. Heat rushed to her cheeks as she quickly set the spoon on the counter and smoothed her hair.

He stepped into the room, and the space suddenly shrunk. While his expression was still amused, something more darkened his eyes. Something that caused her stomach to swirl with anticipation.

"Care to dance?" He held out his hand, his stare never leaving her face.

The feel of his callouses as she slid her palm in his made her heart beat a capriccio. Placing her other hand on his shoulder and having his muscles jump at her touch pushed the music of her heart even faster. He was so hardworking and incredibly strong, and yet, his tenderness and caring surpassed any she'd ever experienced.

He rocked them back in a slow box step. "I'm afraid if I start making music, the windows will break."

She jolted to a stop and glanced to the side at the fur-covered window opening.

"I'm that bad." He gave her a one-sided smile, his dimple tempting her to push up on her toes and kiss it.

While he wasn't completely honest—she'd heard him whistling for the sheep and dogs, and he wasn't that bad—she gave into his tease. The song she picked matched the slow pace of his steps. She didn't want fast when a more dolcissimo song kept her held close.

As they swayed, he pulled her nearer. Here, she was safe. Wrapped in his arms, fear and worry had no hold.

Now, she understood why God put such an emphasis on marriage. She envisioned it was a glimpse into His love for her. She could imagine God's protection so much more clearly. Where before the thought of being covered by God's wings frightened her, stifled her, now she only saw the security intended.

She smiled softly and leaned her head on Otto's shoulder. Burying her face into his neck, she breathed in the smell of drying leaves and fresh air clinging to him. She continued to whistle her song, but the tune faded to a soft hush of wind.

"You seem happy. Are you happy, Klara?" The vulnerability in Otto's whispered question confused her.

Why wouldn't she be overjoyed? She nodded as almost soundless words rushed from her lips.

"I love you, Otto."

He jerked to a stop. The words surprised her as much as they did him. Others back home had complained endlessly about her breathy, barely audible attempts at communication, so she'd forced herself to be silent for the comfort of others. But in the shelter of Otto's arms, she hadn't thought to hold them back.

He pulled away enough to look down at her with such awe that tears blurred her vision. "I heard you. It was soft, like the brush of angel's wings, but I heard you."

She shook her head, stepping back and blinking away the emotion to focus on reality. Her voice was a far cry from angel wings. She tried to put more distance between them, but he held onto her waist.

"Too soft." Her hands signed the words as she whispered. "Hard to hear."

"Not when you're nice and close." He pulled her flush against him, softly spreading his hands wide across her back and searing her skin with his heat. "At this distance, I could listen to you talk for hours."

She rolled her eyes, but the way her breath bottled up in her chest at his teasing negated her bravado.

"Come on, sugar." His lips brushed hers, then skimmed along her jaw, stopping at her ear. "Let me hear the words I've longed for." He kissed right below her ear where her pulse pounded in doppio movimento beneath her skin. "Because there's no way my beautiful, intelligent wife could love me like I love her."

Spearing her hands through his soft hair, she gently tugged him back. She had to look in his eyes, to see if what he said was true. It didn't seem real that God could take her from cowering in a smelly barn to being safe and loved in such a short time. There was no way Otto considered her smart and pretty, loved her like she loved him, when so many others just saw her as a burden.

But when she stared into Otto's eyes, she didn't see smugness nor a hint of annoyance. All that peered back at her was genuine adoration mixed with a heaping amount of vulnerability. His hands trembled as they loosened their hold on her back.

"I love you, Otto." She rushed the quiet words out, sucking in a sob on his name.

His lips stretched into a glorious smile. He ran his thumb over her cheek, then bent his forehead to rest on hers. Their breath hitched and tangled together.

"I love you, too, Klara Lee."

He claimed her lips, searing her with belonging. As day waned to night, the fulfilling of her heart's desire to be truly married slid her happiness to new heights she'd never dreamed of having. Then, as the fire slowly crackled to nothing but embers, they whispered all they held close, all their dreams and hopes, until Otto fell asleep.

Though her eyelids weighed as much as newly chopped logs, she forced them open. She wanted to savor the feel of his arm holding her to him. Relish the rise and fall of his chest beneath her hand. Most of all, she wanted to linger in the peace enveloping her. Because, if life had taught her anything, this serenity—this happiness—couldn't last.

CHAPTER 19

Otto glanced back at the ram slung over his saddle, then at Klara walking next to him. Her cheeks were still pale from her first glimpse of the dead sheep. It was good he'd taken the animal off to the woods to slaughter him. They were out of fresh meat, and this woolly one had been struggling with a recurring leg injury, but Otto didn't want her to have to witness the critter being put down.

Sure, they were ranchers now. He wouldn't be able to protect her from the harder parts of homesteading. He could put it off a bit longer, though, until she grew more accustomed to this life.

She touched his elbow, then began signing.

"What do with sheep's hair?" He watched closely and said each word as her hands moved through the motions.

She nodded.

"Well, I reckon we'll tan the hide."

Her head bobbed in acknowledgment, but she pulled her bottom lip in between her teeth in thought. That small motion tempted him to swoop in and kiss her every single time she did it. He refrained, but just barely. Her hands moved, and he pulled his stare from her lips to her words.

"You want to cut the hair?"

"Yes."

"Why?"

She spelled out y-a-r-n, and his forehead creased.

"You know how to make yarn?" He didn't mean for the question to come out with such disbelief.

Her shoulder lifted in a small shrug, and she nodded. If he could whack himself across the head, he would. She'd had enough people underestimating her in the past. He didn't want to be one of them.

"Sheep book," she signed.

"It tells you how to do that in the sheep book?" He'd read the book Orlando had given him, but since the words jumbling on the page had made it difficult to understand, he'd focused on the sections about animal husbandry.

She smiled. "Yes."

"Huh. Guess I should've read the whole thing instead of just jumping around." He ran his hand along her shoulders, pulled her up next to him, and kissed her on the temple. "Whatever my smart, beautiful wife wants, she gets."

She playfully smacked him on the stomach but didn't pull away. When she wrapped her arm around his back, he wanted nothing more than to be that close forever. Just the two of them, forging their way on the homestead without concern about others.

If only he could push aside his worry about the flock,

then life would be perfect. He rolled his eyes and scoffed at his own childish thoughts. Klara's bright blue eyes peeked up at him.

"Sorry. Just woolgathering."

She lifted one blonde eyebrow in question. Boy howdy, was her face expressive.

"I'm just worrying about the flock, is all." When he didn't continue, she rolled her hand in front of her for him to keep going. "Well, I think the flock is too big. I'm not sure they'll all survive the winter on what we have for grazing around here. I've been thinking about selling some of the animals to the Independence mine up toward Ute City, but I'm concerned."

She held her hand open and shook it side to side. "Why?"

"Well…" He sighed.

If he confessed his reluctance, she'd see that he didn't have a clue what he was doing. He didn't know how to manage a ranch. Definitely wasn't confident enough to make difficult decisions. But, if he wanted to work their ranch together like his father and mother had their farm back in Kansas, he needed to swallow his pride and tell her his concerns.

"What if I cull the flock and we have a hard winter? We could lose enough sheep that the flock wouldn't recover." He stopped Lemy by the trees where he would hang the ram for butchering and slapped the reins to his leg. "But what if we don't have enough food for them to forage, and they die anyways? If we sell now, we'll have money for supplies through the winter, but we might not have any more sheep to sell come spring."

"O.K." Klara signed, then propped her chin on her hand in thought.

"It's a conundrum. I know we need to cull the flock, and selling to the mine is why I moved here instead of somewhere else. But honestly, I've never done anything like this before, and I'm nervous."

There.

He blew out a frustrated breath. Now she knew the truth that her husband didn't have a clue.

"I understand," she signed. "Help me."

She kneeled to the dirt, picked up a stick, and wrote nine hundred. Then she wrote "mine =" and looked up at him with a lift of her eyebrow. He crouched down next to her.

"Well, I was thinking three hundred of the rams could be sold. That would leave a hundred left to mate and keep the flock growing."

She scratched in the dirt five hundred ewes and a hundred rams. Then she struck through two of the zeros on the end of the number leaving only sixty sheep. The number sent his heart right into his stomach. Next, she multiplied thirty by two, then sixty by two and so on until she got over eight hundred. At the bottom, she wrote five years, then shrugged.

"Five years not long," she signed and looked at him.

"Yeah, but it'd be a thin five years." He stood and reached down to help Klara up.

Though he groused, her numbers scratched in the dirt eased a lot of his concerns. The possibility of losing ninety percent of the flock existed, sure, but it'd take a mighty big catastrophe to drop that many. Even so, five years for them to get back on their feet, and Klara had only accounted for single births, not twins and triplets like so many ewes had delivered.

She let him help her up, then stepped up to him. Her palm patted his chest, and her lips pressed a kiss on his cheek.

"You're a smart man, Otto Lee," she whispered faintly against his ear. "Stop doubting yourself."

He pulled away just enough to look into her eyes. All he saw was trust and encouragement. He kissed her softly on the lips then leaned his forehead against hers.

"God sure sent me a blessing when He gave me you, Klara. Never imagined finding a wife the way I did, but I'd stand against any enemy a hundred times over if it meant I got you."

Her smile pressed against his lips, radiating her joy. Helpmate couldn't be a more perfect term for what she was to him. With her by his side and God's leading, Otto felt he could withstand anything the wild Rockies threw at them.

CHAPTER 20

OTTO SLOWED Lemy as they entered Fryingpan Town. Klara's hands trembled against his waist where she held on. When he'd suggested the night before that they go to church before they stop in at the store, she'd gone as white as the new snow covering Mount Sopris's peak. She hadn't said anything, just gave a terse nod and bent back over the book she'd been reading. While he doubted the Müller's would be at church, Otto understood her anxiety.

"I don't think you have to worry about running into those polecats in church. They didn't strike me as the worshipping type." Otto pressed his palm over her hands.

"Not them." Her whisper almost got lost in the noise of Lemy's steps and the waking town.

"Then why are you shaking like a jackrabbit?"

She rested her forehead against his back. Her shrug didn't give him any clue, either. Her lack of explanation swirled in his stomach like strong coffee kept on the fire too long. If something else had happened in town, he needed to know.

"Klara, sugar, please tell me what's wrong." He bent to the side so he could see her.

"People don't like me." Klara signed the simple sentence.

"They just don't know you." He placed his hand around hers.

She shook her head and slapped his hand away. Then she snatched her paper from her pocket and wrote in tiny, neat letters.

"Never like me. Not back home. Not here. No one wants to waste time on a dumb mute."

She shoved the notepad into his hand and crossed her arms. His heart sank with each word. She'd told him about not having any friends and how even her mother hadn't taken the time to learn to communicate with her. Her talk of the past had been nonchalant, but maybe there was more to it than just being lonely.

"You are far from dumb. If people don't want to take the time to learn that, then it's their loss." He took her hand when she let loose a disbelieving laugh. "If people at the church aren't welcoming, we just won't go back."

"O.K." She signed in his palm.

"Okay," he repeated.

As he urged Lemy forward, he threaded his fingers through hers. He couldn't imagine anyone not loving Klara the moment they met her. She had such a kind spirit. Yet, he also knew people could be mighty judgmental when it came to things they didn't understand. He wouldn't force her to be around people who wouldn't even take the time to find out who she really was.

When they stopped in front of the teeny log church, she clenched his fingers tighter. He swung off the saddle, then gently lifted her down. Her gaze darted around the church and street like a deer that smelled a predator.

Leaning in so only she could hear him, he whispered, "I'm not gonna let anyone hurt you, Klara. I promise."

She closed her eyes and gave a small nod.

"Let's go inside." He offered her his elbow and smiled.

She didn't set her hand daintily on his arm. No, she gripped his sleeve like a bear clawing a kill. He patted her hand, but she didn't ease her fingers. A tall, scrawny man with glasses, maybe ten years Otto's senior, waited by the door.

"Welcome. It's so nice to see new faces." He smiled broadly and reached out his hand. "I'm Pastor James. You're the first to arrive today."

When Klara didn't let go of Otto's arm, he patted her hand again. She uncurled her fingers, a pink blush blooming on her cheeks.

"Otto and Klara Lee, sir. It's a pleasure to meet you." Otto clasped the outstretched hand as the man's eyes brightened.

"Oh, the newlyweds." He shook Otto's hand harder. "Dr. Jones told us about Trapper Dan's street-side ceremony." Pastor James *tsked* and turned to Klara with a good-hearted smile. "That man keeps taking all the fun out of my job. That's the second marriage he's stolen right from under my nose."

Klara returned his smile with a trembling one of her own and mouthed, "Sorry."

"Don't trouble yourself. I'm just jealous I wasn't the one to bind you two in holy matrimony." He motioned to the door behind them. "I'm very honored you have come to join us in worship. We're a small lot that gathers, but it's good to fellowship, no matter the numbers."

"We're glad to be here." Otto took Klara's hand and led her in.

When they crossed the threshold, she gasped and pulled her hand from his. His gaze darted around the small space searching for trouble. Nothing was there except ten pews, a pulpit, and a piano. Klara's eyes widened as she stepped toward the piano. She ran a reverent hand over the top of it, then along the keys.

"Does your wife play, Mr. Lee?" A soft voice startled him from his staring at his wife to a tiny woman about his age standing next to him.

His ears heated, wondering how long she'd witnessed him gawking.

"I ... I don't know," he croaked.

"Well, we'll have to remedy that." The woman stepped away before Otto could stop her.

For a tiny thing, she moved fast. By the time Otto caught up to her, she was already talking.

"It's a beauty, isn't it?" the woman asked Klara who nodded in answer. "The family that brought it out here went back east after the wife passed away. The husband left the thing with us. Said he couldn't stand to look at it anymore. Shame really. It's quite a beautiful instrument."

In truth, Otto hadn't seen a piano like it since leaving Kansas. Most pianos in the area were upright ones in saloons. Bringing a baby grand across the Rockies had to have been quite a feat.

"Do you play?" The woman asked Klara.

Klara nodded.

"Splendid. All I'm good at is plinking the keys like a child." She chuckled. "Oh, where are my manners. I'm Pastor James's wife, Betty, and you must be Klara Lee."

Klara nodded again, her smile genuine as she reached out her hand. Otto eased himself into the front pew, determined to step in if necessary, but wanting Klara to have room to see the acceptance this woman was offering.

"Wonderful to meet you, darling." Betty took both Klara's hands in hers, then ushered her onto the piano bench. "I've picked songs for today's service and have them here on this scrap of paper. Why don't you look them over and see if we need to change any of them out for ones you know."

Klara opened the fraying hymnal like it was a holy relic. After finding the correct page, she carefully set it in the holder and placed her fingers on the keys. Otto held his breath as she sat still except for her fingers sliding over the ivory. Then, with a deep sigh like she'd been without air for months, Klara played.

Otto had never heard the familiar hymn *All Hail the Power of Jesus' Name* performed in such a way. Her fingers flew through the notes, adding layers upon the normal ones in a mastery he'd never witnessed before. Her eyes closed halfway through the song, and the sun chose that moment to shine through the window. She was an angel, haloed in light and song.

When she finished, Otto felt a keen sense of loss, like he'd just experienced a truly special moment. Clapping started behind him, jerking Klara's eyes opened. Her cheeks flushed at the same time as the rest of her paled. Otto turned to see all the pews full of rundown men, most teary-eyed.

"Yes, I think she'll do splendidly." Betty patted Otto on the arm, a cunning smile on her face as Pastor James walked to the pulpit and asked everyone to join in song. "I do hope you and your lovely wife will join us for dinner after church, Mr. Lee."

"Sure. Yes. We'd love to." Otto stumbled out the words as the pastor bowed his head in prayer.

While Pastor James thanked God for the awe-inspiring music, Otto watched as Klara's eyes darted around the church, finally landing on him. He smiled and winked at her in encouragement. As far as church introductions went, he'd never had one so melodious.

CHAPTER 21

Klara's heart hadn't stopped banging like a bass drum in a marching band since she'd opened her eyes and found a room full of men staring at her. Now with Mrs. Betty dragging Klara to the parsonage, her pulse's staccato beat might be too much for her to handle. Her gaze darted to Otto as he jogged down the boardwalk. He'd spotted the man he was supposed to talk to about the sheep and wanted to catch up with him, leaving Klara in the hands of a stranger.

The fear that gripped Klara was uncalled for. Truly. She *knew* that. The pastor's wife had been nothing but kind since Klara joined her and Otto on the front pew. But knowing that in her head didn't keep her heart in check. Lots of people had been kind to Klara in public when judging eyes watched.

"Now, Klara dear, I pray you'll consider playing every Sunday for us." Mrs. Betty patted Klara's hand she'd threaded through her arm. "Your playing is a gift straight from the gates of Heaven. Why, I don't think even the angels can play as beautifully as you."

Klara looked at the woman and raised her eyebrow in skepticism.

"Well, you're right. That might be a bit of a tall tale." Mrs. Betty's eyes sparkled. "But you most definitely would have their halos trembling with joy at being able to join in worship with you. Please tell me you'll do it."

Klara chuckled at Mrs. Betty's cunning flattery. It warmed her heart to know that her music was appreciated and wanted. Klara liked the spunky woman who couldn't be more than five years Klara's senior. She reminded Klara of what an older sister or cousin might have been like. Yet, memories of her past also needled along her scalp, making her weary of agreeing. She pushed off her reluctance to lose this budding friendship and pulled out her paper and pencil.

"Must ask Otto, Mrs. Betty." She took care to write each letter clearly and quickly.

She held her breath as she showed Mrs. Betty. Would the woman's frustration show immediately when she realized Klara couldn't speak? Would her face flit with disgust like so many others had?

"Yes, you're smart to ask your husband. Makes them feel like they're in charge, but from the look of love and adoration on his face while you played, I'm sure he'll agree." Mrs. Betty squeezed Klara's arm against her body. "And dear, if we are to be the best of friends, you must just call me Betty. None of this missus nonsense."

Friends? Klara had never had one, especially not a best friend. Her face hurt as her mouth pushed her cheeks up.

"Betty," Klara mouthed.

"Great. Now that that is settled, you can help me make up a batch of drop biscuits to go with the stew. I'm afraid I got caught up in my sewing this morning and didn't watch the time close enough."

Betty's words sank the joy from Klara's heart into her stomach, like the times they'd traveled the mountain passes and the wagon tipped precariously close to the steep drop-offs. What would Betty think when she found out that not only could Klara not talk, but she couldn't cook? She sighed and scratched out her message. Might as well get it over with. Disappointment was easier when joy didn't have time to fly too high.

"Never learned to cook," Betty read the note out loud. "Truly?"

Klara shrugged and nodded.

"Well, we'll have to remedy that, won't we?"

"Really?" Klara mouthed, shocked that Betty truly didn't care.

"Absolutely, dear. It's one of the secret ways we wives can influence our husbands." Betty rushed Klara into the small log cabin next to the church. "When you have something important to talk to him about, fluffy warm biscuits or a sweet pie will do wonders to ease him into agreement. And if you can figure out his favorite treat, it'll work better than Aphrodite's love potion."

She winked, and Klara's cheeks heated to an inferno. Was this truly what friends talked about? She placed a hand on her hot skin.

"I see I've scandalized you." Betty handed a mixing bowl to Klara. "I wish I could say it's the lack of female companionship that has my mouth running faster than a miner who found gold, but I've always been somewhat of a blunt person. Drove my mama to fits, but it drew my James to me like a bear to honey."

Betty bumped her shoulder against Klara's.

"He said it was refreshing knowing what was on a woman's mind. There've been times in our marriage I'm sure he's regretted confessing that. Now, take out that handy notepad of yours. I'm going to give you my secret drop biscuit recipe that will have that husband of yours begging for more than just seconds."

Betty winked then pulled the flour canister from a shelf. Laughter shook Klara's shoulders, and a blush almost continually heated her ears, but she loved every moment spent in Betty's kitchen. She took detailed notes, determined to learn how to create biscuits that would make Otto's mouth water. In truth, the recipe wasn't difficult.

Neither was the friendship.

Betty urged Klara to ask questions. They chatted about recipes, sewing, and music. The conversation moved so fast that Klara's hand cramped and her handwriting grew messy. Never once did she feel like the scratching of her pencil irritated Betty. By the time Otto and James joined them, Klara knew deep within her heart that Betty was someone she'd cherish all the days of her life.

CHAPTER 22

SHEEP BLEATED LOUDLY as Otto pushed them toward Ute City. River Daniels was meeting Otto halfway, but the miles seemed to plod on forever. Truly, it was barely past midday, but Otto itched to get home to Klara.

He didn't like leaving her at the cabin alone and was surprised when she had insisted she stay behind. It wasn't safe, even with Baron keeping guard. Otto shook his head at the half-truth and motioned at Duke to move the sheep faster. Klara was just as safe at home as any other frontierswoman. Maybe a bit safer, in fact, with Baron protecting her. They hadn't had any visitors out at the property, and since moving to Trapper Dan's place, no one knew where their homestead was.

Still, leaving Klara behind didn't sit right. He'd left the rifle, but could she use it? He shifted in the saddle as his stomach knotted. All this fretting did nothing but give him indigestion.

A sharp whistle up ahead snapped Otto's attention forward and his hand to his holster. River Daniels waved from a knoll, then motioned to the men with him. The men split up, circling the sheep, while River galloped toward Otto.

"Duke, come," Otto hollered at the dog and pulled Lemy to a stop as River neared.

Finally, Otto could head back. If they hurried, they might make it home before dark. River stopped beside Otto and reached out his hand.

"Appreciate you meeting us." River's black hair braided down his back made the Ute in him more prominent.

It surprised Otto, with all the hostility toward the Utes, the man would be given a position over others. But River's father's reputation as a hunter and guide must have eased the concerns. Amazing how prejudices could be put aside when it benefited those who normally hated.

Otto never put much stock in the color of a person's skin. He'd seen just as much harm come at the hands of whites. Better to judge a person by their actions than their skin.

"My pleasure." Otto nodded his chin at the sheep. "Three hundred rams should be a nice addition to whatever you hunt up."

River leaned his forearm on the saddle horn. "Might not be an addition. Game is harder and harder to find. Too many animals have been slaughtered to keep the herds healthy."

The declaration chilled Otto to his core. No game would mean the men holing up for winter in Fryingpan Town would get hungry. If men got desperate, his remaining herd wouldn't be safe.

"You're not right in town, are you?" River asked, like he'd read Otto's mind.

"No. We're several miles outside in an area protected by cottonwoods." A frigid breeze blew down Otto's collar. "I drove the sheep well around the town on the way up."

"Good." River nodded. "I'm sure people already know you have them, but if you can keep your homestead private, you shouldn't have any problems." He shrugged. "Just might want to take different paths home so it's harder to follow."

Otto mulled the thought over. He hadn't even considered that. He'd been so focused on getting the sheepfold set up and taking them to graze as far each day as he could. Worrying about someone following them home to steal from them hadn't even entered his mind.

"Thanks." Otto needed to get home to Klara. All this talk of desperate men had his already bunched nerves on fire.

"Anything for a friend of Orlando's."

The comment momentarily stopped Otto's fretting. "You know Orlando?"

"Our families have been friends since before either of us was born." River smiled, but it didn't reach his eyes. "I've spent countless days with the Thomas family. Reckoned I'd marry one of his sisters, but that wasn't to be."

River stared out across the sheep. Otto had heard from Dan that Orlando's sister, Beatrice, had disappeared. She'd been attacked by one of the Sweeney's, and Dan assumed she was dead. They never found her body, which was a shame. More than likely an animal had gotten to her.

"Well, you need to be paid, and we need to move this flock up the valley." River forced a smile and reached into his pocket. "As promised, three dollars a head. The mine would like the first chance to purchase from the flock in the spring."

Otto took the pouch and shoved it in his duster's inner pocket. He'd never held nine hundred dollars before. He wasn't relieved like he thought he would be. No, having this much cash made him itchier, like any minute someone would jump from the bushes and gun him down.

Then what would happen to Klara?

"Much obliged." He reached his hand out to River. "We'll see how the winter is on the flock, but if I'm culling, I'll contact the mine first."

"I'll be around if you need anything." River touched the brim of his hat and turned his horse.

Otto watched for several minutes to make sure no sheep turned back to follow him. Each second dragged like oozing sap. With the money heavy against his chest and concern for Klara gripping his heart, he turned Lemy's head toward home the instant the last sheep was out of sight.

"Come on, boys. Let's go home." Otto motioned to Duke.

He set Lemy's pace at a fast walk. Logically, he knew Klara most likely hadn't come to any harm. Injuring Lemy over foolish fretting would put his family in even more of a precarious position. The horses at the livery weren't cheap and weren't even half the horse Lemy was.

At first, he distracted himself with what to do with the money. They'd need to find a place to hide it. He didn't want it in the cabin. The space was small, and hiding spots were too obvious. He had a tin canister he stored extra nails and odd bits of metal he picked up in. It was possible the can would fit in the hole he'd found in one of the cottonwoods. They could keep enough out to get them through a few months, then hide the rest.

With that decided and still several miles to go, he thought about Klara. She'd already read through the sheep book Orlando had given Otto. She'd pointed out ways they could use the wool and how selling yarn might be just as profitable as the animal itself. He closed his eyes and imagined the blisters she'd gotten on her fingertips from trying to spin the wool. When he'd told her to slow down, that she had all winter to learn, she'd glared up at him and kept going.

He liked that she no longer cowered or flinched in fear. In fact, her sass made his heart trot just as much as her kisses did. Well, almost as much.

No matter her newfound strength, she still was too small. Her time with the Müllers had left its toll on her body. She'd never be able to defend herself if someone had malicious intent.

And that brought Otto right back to the fretting he'd worked so hard to leave on the trail behind. As if Lemy sensed Otto's distress, the horse picked up his pace. It could have been that the horse knew home was close, which meant his feed was not far away. Whatever the case, Otto gave Lemy the reins and let him fly.

Pounding hooves ate up the distance like his tail was on fire. Duke yipped beside Lemy, a smile on his face as he raced to keep up. The cold air rushed by and stung Otto's eyes, making them water.

When he got close to the homestead, he pulled on the reins. No use scaring Klara by surging in. The door swung open, and Klara emerged with the rifle at the ready.

He laughed and slowed Lemy to a walk. Looks like he didn't need to worry about his wife after all. She rested the gun across her arms and scanned the area behind him.

When he got close, she scowled up at him and signed, "Why run?"

"Because I missed you."

He slid off the saddle and wrapped his arms around her, gun and all. He kissed her long and hard, relishing that she returned his fervor. A blast of chilled air hit them, and she shivered.

"Go get warmed. I'll take care of Lemy and be right inside." He spoke against her lips.

She nodded, gave him another kiss that had him curling his toes in his cowboy boots to stay standing and went inside. He rushed through his chores with Lemy, doing what needed to be done but not lingering like normal. Lemy didn't seem to mind since Otto put extra grain in the bucket.

When he pushed open the cabin door, tantalizing aromas welcomed him. His gaze skittered from the bowls of thick stew steaming on the table to the plate of golden biscuits beckoning in the middle and finally landing on the pie oozing sticky goodness onto the counter. His mouth watered as he crossed to Klara twisting her hands in her apron.

"This looks delicious." He kissed her cheek. "You did all this today?"

She nodded and handed him her notepad.

"Betty gave you some recipes you wanted to try." His forehead furrowed as he glanced up at Klara. "That's why you wanted to stay home?"

She mouthed, "yes" and motioned for his chair. After

he said a blessing, thanking God for the safe travels, the sale of the sheep, and the meal, she stared at him as he buttered his biscuit and took a bite. He closed his eyes and groaned in pleasure at the flaky goodness melting in his mouth.

"Klara, sugar, you make biscuits like these every day, and I'll be one happy man." He opened his eyes to see hers sparkling with playfulness.

"Good," she mouthed and plucked a piece of biscuit into her own mouth. "Very good."

He didn't think she was talking about the bread, and he wasn't about to ask. All he wanted was to enjoy the amazing food his lovely wife had created and then enjoy his lovely wife. He had an entire day away from her he had to make up.

"You know what?" He tossed his biscuit onto his plate. "Food can wait."

He scooped Klara up from her chair and stalked to the bed. Her mouth gaped, and her shoulders shook in laughter. He caught her joy with his kiss, and she tasted sweeter than anything he'd ever had.

CHAPTER 23

When Otto kissed Klara on the cheek in front of the general store, she was tempted to grab his duster and drag him into the store with her. She didn't want to go by herself. The sentiment left her feeling like a scared child rather than the grown woman she finally felt she'd become. Forcing a smile, she stepped away.

"If you finish before I get back, head on over to Betty's. Go straight there. No sightseeing." Otto's jaw clenched as he squeezed her hand.

She raised an eyebrow and looked up and down the clapboard and tent town. He followed her survey, glaring when his gaze landed on the saloon with men already loitering at ten in the morning. If she didn't push Otto along, he would stay with her. Then how would she prove herself a strong woman able to handle situations?

She patted his shoulder, kissed his cheek, then mouthed, "No sightseeing."

With a curt nod, he swung up onto Lemy's back and touched his brim. For a moment, she watched him head to the livery, taking in his broad shoulders and strong back. That was a sight she didn't mind seeing over and over again. A man brushed past her, chuckling low, and her face heated at being caught gawking.

She adjusted the basket on her arm and stepped into the store. The mix of leather, spices, and vinegar from the pickle jar hit her nose, making her stomach turn. A disheveled man smelling of stale alcohol and sweat pushed past her. Her knees trembled and vision blurred.

She swallowed and held her breath until she reached the fabric bolts lined up in the corner. Taking her handkerchief from her sleeve, she dotted her sweaty forehead. This was not the woman she wanted to be, becoming faint and nauseous so easily.

Fingering the calico and canvas to regain her bearings, she took deep breaths and let her gaze search the store. If she could locate the items on her list while hiding by the fabric, then she could beeline for the supplies and get to Betty's without any more incidents. Mentally checking her list, she found most of what she needed and headed across the store.

Two women hung around the thread. When they glanced over, Klara smiled. It quickly faded when they turned away without returning the gesture and whispered among themselves. The hair on the back of her neck stood on end as she made her way to the canned goods. Why would they act like that? She'd never met them before.

As quick as she could, she gathered items from her list. With her basket heavy with canned tomatoes, Magic Yeast, One Spoon baking powder, and a tin of oolong tea, she weaved her way to the counter. She made sure to smile as pleasantly as she could at the man behind the counter, even though he glared at her.

Pushing her notepad across the counter, she pointed to the items still on her list and mouthed, "Please."

The man rolled his eyes, grumbling as he read. Her stomach turned again, and her gaze darted to a pair of men watching her from where they sat at a checkerboard set on a barrel. They shook their heads in disgust and leaned over the barrel. Klara patted her clammy forehead as her nerves skittered like spiders along her skin.

"How much do you want?" The storekeeper asked loudly and slowly, like she was hard of hearing instead of mute.

She jerked at his abrupt manner and pulled the notepad back to herself. Her hand trembled so hard she could hardly write. She'd figured they'd be in bags on the shelf for her to choose from, but they weren't. She had already calculated how much flour, sugar, and coffee they'd need, but having never shopped for groceries before, she had no clue what sizes the items came in.

"Come on." The man groused, tapping his finger on the counter. "I ain't got all day."

She scratched out her question and turned it to him.

"What are the quantities?" He read her note aloud. "Are you daft? I've got however much you need."

His sharp tone had her face burning with humiliation. She wanted to dump the items on the counter and storm out. However, with this being the only store in town, she couldn't. Holding in a scowl, she pushed her pencil across the paper.

"Lady, I don't have time to waste watching you scribble like a halfwit."

"Horace Jenty," Pastor James's deep voice boomed behind Klara, making her nearly jump out of her skin. "I'm sure I didn't just hear you accosting Mrs. Lee."

Pastor James's eyebrow rose just slightly. Fire burned in his eyes like it had on Sunday when he'd preached about the danger of sin. He stepped up beside Klara and turned the paper to read it.

"By the looks of it, you might be the halfwit if you can't read a simple grocery list." He spun the paper back to Horace. "It's clear as day that Mrs. Lee needs five pounds of flour and sugar and one pound of coffee."

Horace grumbled as he turned to the barrels behind him and started scooping flour into a burlap bag. Klara's hand shook as she reached for her paper and slid it into her pocket. Pastor James turned to peer outside.

"Chin up, Klara. You can't show these small-minded people who you really are all tucked in like a roly-poly," Pastor James whispered for only her to hear.

She peeked up at him. He nodded, and she pulled her shoulders back. As Horace stomped back to the counter with her items, she held his glare with a look of determination of her own. As he mumbled amounts of the items he pointed at, she added the amount in her head and fingered her money. He looked at her with a smirk.

"That'll be—"

She slapped the exact amount needed on the counter before he could finish. He counted the money, his eyebrows winging to his forehead when it was correct. His mouth flapped like a trout out of water as he gaped at her. Satisfaction washed over her, pulling her lips up on one side.

"Proverbs 10:18 says, 'He that hideth hatred with lying

lips, and he that uttereth a slander, is a fool.'" Pastor James knocked on the counter, then scanned the people watching. "I'm sure you don't want to be fools and believe everything liars spread."

A pregnant silence filled the store. It pushed against Klara, threatening to bend her shoulders again. But she was done being humiliated by others' opinions.

Pastor James handed Horace a list and, after saying he'd return later for it, invited Klara to have tea with Betty. Klara kept her gaze forward as he led her to the door, not daring to look at the customers gawking. Obviously, the Müllers weren't done making her life miserable.

CHAPTER 24

OTTO WRAPPED Lemy's reins around the hitching post in front of the parsonage. Music pounded from the church's piano, so he veered his feet there. The song rushed over notes with a loud hammering tune that bombarded his nerves. The thundering vibrations rose up his throat, creating a sense of foreboding he couldn't explain. It was just music, and yet, the unease in his spirit quickened his pace.

When he opened the door, Pastor James straightened from his lean against the wall, a staying hand lifting to stop Otto. James's shoulders relaxed when he saw Otto, his hand dropping to his side. Klara's stormy music barreled over Otto, knocking him in the chest.

"What happened?" he asked James, not taking his eyes off his wife bent over the keys.

"Step outside and talk with me for a minute." James placed his hand on Otto's shoulder.

Otto tore his gaze from Klara and speared James with a glare.

James lifted his hand from Otto's shoulder in surrender. "Just a minute. I promise."

With one last glance at Klara with her eyes closed and fingers racing across the keys, Otto turned back outside. The second the door clicked shut, he spun.

"What happened?" He forced the words through gritted teeth.

"It seems the Müllers have been spreading rumors about Klara." James shook his head in disappointment. "The livery owner's wife visited Betty earlier today, all in a tizzy about how the marshal should arrest the mute thief even if she's dumber than a rock."

No wonder the livery owner had acted strange around Otto. Anger blasted hot in Otto's chest. He clenched his teeth to keep the curses from flying on church property. He wasn't one for profanity, but the words tumbled up his throat and across his tongue so fast he almost didn't have time to swallow them.

"I know. I know." James's hard eyes speared Otto. "Betty sure laid into the woman. Said Klara was the most talented and intelligent woman she'd ever met. Said anyone who would believe people the likes of the Müllers were the ones with the smarts of a rock."

The picture of Betty saying that burst a laugh from Otto. "How'd that go over?"

James smiled with pride. "Betty said the woman took a good ten seconds for the statement to sink in before she spurted in indignation and stormed out."

The support of James and Betty cooled Otto's anger to a simmer instead of a rage. The music blasting through the thick log church walls riled it back up. He tipped his chin toward the door and raised a questioning eyebrow at James.

"Horace at the store gave Klara a hard time. Seems he believed the Müllers, too." James shrugged.

Otto wasn't okay with that simple answer. "What happened exactly?"

As James recounted the exchange, Otto's fist clenched tighter and tighter by his side. He gritted his teeth so hard pain spiked his temple. He took a step toward the general store. No one treated his wife like that without consequences.

James's hand landed on Otto's shoulder. "No, Otto. Leave him be for now."

Otto jerked his shoulder out of James's grip. "You'd let someone treat Betty like that? The man deserves the lesson a good punch in the face would teach."

"If you go over there, you'll undo everything that Klara proved." James's words didn't make a lick of sense.

"How?"

Otto crossed his arms. He'd give James time to explain. Horace wasn't going anywhere.

"Klara didn't cower or cry. She held her chin up high. Before Horace even told her how much she owed, she slapped the exact amount on the counter and then stalked out of there with the dignity of a queen." James grinned in satisfaction, then sobered. "If the people of this town are ever going to see Klara in a different light, she has to prove it. You going around pummeling people isn't going to ingratiate anyone to her *or* you. Then the Müllers win."

Otto's chest heaved with the injustice. Was it too much to ask that the snakes would slink away and let Klara be?

They'd already hurt and used her. Why try to ruin her reputation now after weeks of nothing?

"Go to your wife, Otto. There will be plenty of time to prove who she truly is." James clapped Otto on the shoulder and strode toward the parsonage. "Just lock the door. People keep coming in to listen."

Otto pushed the church door open and locked it behind him. Walking past the pews, Otto prayed to God for words to say to make this better. Klara's music didn't let up but washed over Otto in waves of emotion. The anger was there, but layered beneath that, he heard the hurt. It clogged his throat and stung his eyes.

He sat next to her on the piano bench, facing the opposite way. She didn't look at him, but the pounding of the keys slowed. She sniffed, her fingers softly transforming the song from anger to a slow, sad melody.

"James says I can't pummel the jerk for what he did." Otto groaned and leaned his back against the piano. "Says it'll make things worse."

His leaning made a discordant clang of the keys that interrupted her song and stilled her fingers. He was glad he chose to sit this way so he could watch her expressions. He crossed his arms, attempting to pretend to pout.

"I'm not sure if I like James and his logic much anymore."

That brought a small lift of Klara's lips. She pulled her fingers off the piano and finally looked at him. The pain in her eyes speared right to his chest.

"I'm so sorry, sugar. They'll learn, in time ,the Müllers are nothing but cold-hearted liars." He reached up and ran the back of his fingers across her cheek. "That you are smart, sweet, and the most perfect woman ever created."

She rolled her eyes, though they sparkled with tears at his words. Whether from sadness or hope, he couldn't tell. He would do everything he could to make sure if she started crying from grief, her day would end in hope.

"Let's go home, wife." He leaned forward and pressed a soft kiss to her lips. "We're not slinking off either."

He shook his head, stood, then helped her up. She lifted an eyebrow at him. He kissed her again.

"Nope. We're riding straight through town with our heads high and backs straight. It'll take a lot more than a few nasty lies to break us, right?"

"Us?" She mouthed, surprise and doubt on her face.

"We face life's joys and struggles together, Klara." Otto grabbed her hand. "That's what it means to love."

A smile bloomed wide across her face a moment before she threw herself into his arms. He held her close, putting all his love and devotion into his kiss. Who cared what others thought as long as he had Klara and God by his side?

CHAPTER 25

Klara dug through the trunk with one hand while she blew on the burn on her other. Searching for the liniment would be much easier with both. Served her right for being distracted while cooking. She barely had a handle on preparing food without scorching it. Why did she ever think she could spin yarn, read the book on shepherding, and cook at the same time?

She pushed a blanket out of the way. A thunk landed beside her, causing her to jump. The door slammed against the wall, and her heart jolted into her throat.

"Sorry," Otto grunted as he hauled an armful of wood in. "I bumped the door a little too hard."

Klara slumped against the trunk, her hand over her heart to hold the pounding in her chest. Otto hooked the door with his foot, pushed it closed, and then, after stacking the wood, latched the lock. Klara loved watching him work and how his body moved with ease and grace, though it contained so much strength. She shook her head and turned to the mess she'd made.

"What's going on?" Otto crossed the room and kneeled next to her.

She held up her hand and cringed.

Otto hissed. "That's a good one. How'd you burn the back of your hand?"

She made two signs, embarrassed.

"Reading and cooking?" Otto's lips twitched.

She signed another, and Otto's eyebrows raised to his hairline.

"And spinning?" He chuckled and shook his head, the sound coiling warmth in her stomach. "I'm all for getting the most out of your time, but maybe three activities at once might be one too many."

She shrugged and signed, "Maybe. I didn't ruin supper."

"Well, that's good, at least." Otto gave her a look of false relief. "I'm not sure if I could stomach another of your burnt offerings after the food has been so good."

She gasped and swatted his shoulder with her uninjured hand. He grabbed it and kissed her palm. Her heart picked up its pace again. At this rate, she'd wear it out at a young age.

"Let's get your burn treated so we can eat." Otto picked up the fabric she'd pushed out of the trunk, revealing a book beneath.

Klara sucked in her breath and reached a shaky hand to her father's journal. In the chaos of leaving the Müllers and the busyness of adjusting to married life, she hadn't opened her bag from where she'd stuffed it. How could she have forgotten she had something so precious?

"What's that?" Otto pushed the fabric into the trunk, closed the lid, and then helped Klara up.

"My father's book," she signed.

"Like a journal?" Otto asked, and she was reminded again just how smart her husband was.

He'd picked up on the signs she used quickly and was able to fill in the gaps on the words he didn't know. The only other person who she'd been able to talk with was her father, and even he hadn't picked it up as fast as Otto.

She nodded, sat on the trunk, and ran a hand over the leather cover. When she'd been with the Müllers, the pain of losing her parents had kept her from reading it. Then, the pain gave way to exhaustion from slaving for the wicked couple and avoiding Hildebert. Both made reading next to impossible. But forgetting about it completely tore at her heart.

"What a blessing it is that you still have that." Otto's soft, pained words jerked her teary eyes from the journal to his face. "I don't have anything of my family's. When Pa and I left Kansas, we only took what could fit in our saddlebags."

Otto hadn't ever talked about what had happened to his pa. She could tell talking about him was painful, so she had let it be. She held her breath, praying he'd tell her. As he stared at her father's journal, he opened his mouth, paused, then snapped it shut with a sharp shake of his head. When he finally lifted his eyes to hers, they held such regret and sadness her breath caught.

"Let's get your burn doctored up and eat so you can get to reading." He gave her a melancholy smile. "I'm sure your pa's journal will be much more enthralling than a book on sheep."

They weren't the words she wanted to hear, but she wouldn't push Otto for more. If he didn't want to talk about his family, she couldn't fault him. There wasn't much in her past she wanted to dredge through, either.

All through supper, her gaze strayed to the journal. What would she find there? Had her father written his hopes and dreams, or would it simply be filled with plans and lists? Once he had made the decision to move west, Vati wrote in the thing every night while they lounged in the parlor. Her mother had groused about him annoying her with his scratching. Klara had simply rolled her eyes, since she often heard that complaint with her own notes she'd scrawled to her mother. The memories of those evenings made her chest ache.

Otto dragged a chunk of bread across the bottom of the bowl, sopping up every last drop of the stew. She smiled as he popped the bite into his mouth and leaned back in his chair with a contented sigh.

"You sure outdid yourself tonight, sugar." He patted his stomach. "I'm fuller than a sheep who gorged on spring clover."

She shook her head, chuckling in satisfaction, and stood to clear the dishes. The sooner she finished the chore, the sooner she could read her father's journal. Her gut twisted, part in anticipation, but also in apprehension. She wasn't sure which emotion was stronger.

When she reached for the bowls, Otto touched her hand. "I'll take care of these, Klara. Go sit with your Pa."

Otto's voice held such longing, she slid onto his lap and buried her face into the crook of his neck. He clung to her like she was the most precious treasure, holding her so tightly against him she almost couldn't breathe. She didn't mind the sensation, not when her own body trembled with grief and pain. They had both lost everything, yet at her lowest point, God had sent Otto.

"Thank you for rescuing me that day, for giving me life," she whispered against his neck.

He shook his head and pulled her even closer. "No, you're the one who gave me life, Klara. Life, hope, family, love. All of the things I never thought I'd have again."

She pulled back and touched his cheek. Her smile trembled. How could one feel such heartache yet intense jubilation at the same time? She pressed her lips tenderly to his and sighed.

"I love you." The small words didn't seem enough for what she felt.

"I love you, too," he whispered against her mouth. He gave her another squeeze then pushed her off his lap. "Lord Almighty, woman, you can't keep distracting me. I've got dishes to clean."

She grinned as she swatted Otto's hands. He stood and reached for the bowls, but she wrapped him in another hug. She kissed his chest where his generous heart was.

"Thank you." She glanced up at him.

He pressed his lips to her forehead. "Anything for you."

Sitting back in her chair, she grabbed the journal and turned to the first entry. Her father's neat handwriting brought fresh tears to her eyes. Reading the opening prayer he'd written for guidance, wisdom, and protection slipped the tears across her cheeks, and she worried she wouldn't be strong enough to read any further. Had it been God's plan for them to go West or was the death and heartache evidence of Vati's folly?

Did it matter?

Klara closed her eyes and shook her head. No, it

didn't. The past couldn't be changed, only learned from. She couldn't do that with her eyes pressed shut.

With a nod and quick prayer for strength, she forged ahead. The following entries laid out her father's investigation into which area to move to. He'd had such hope for this new beginning, not only for his success but for her as well. Every few entries a sentence with her name would pop up, and she'd see anew her father's dreams for her. He'd imagined the move was a chance for her to find happiness the pretentious members of society in Ohio never would afford her. The move was his opportunity to bring their family closer together.

Too bad it had destroyed them.

She glanced at Otto where he sat at the table, sharpening the knives. Yet out of the ashes of that destruction, her father's dream of her finding happiness had emerged. Prayers had been answered.

Turning the page, she read the next entry with a sense of rightness in her heart. Sitting up straighter, she read the words again. Details of her father's property purchases filled the page. Not only had he bought land outside of Fryingpan Town to build a house on, he had also acquired a storefront in town to set up his law office. Her father described everything from who he bought the land from to how much he'd spent. He even had drawn a decent map of where the properties were located.

"Otto!" Klara gasped and shoved the journal to him.

His eyebrows furrowed as he scanned the words. As he read, she scratched her own questions down on her notepad. Did she have a claim to the property? Could they sell the property in town and use the funds to build a house of their own? Could they even find out the answers? When he looked up from the journal, she pushed her note to him.

"I reckon you'd be the owner, that is, if your pa had a will with you as the beneficiary." He traced his finger over the drawn map. "I know which building this is. Your pa knew how to pick 'em, not that he had many options."

Klara nodded. He'd always been blessed with good business and investing sense. It was how he'd amassed the wealth they'd had.

"Finding the answers might be difficult, especially with winter coming." He shrugged.

"Can we post letters?" She signed.

She could write to the land agent mentioned in her father's journal, maybe even send a letter to her father's old partner back in Ohio. Surely one of them would be able to help.

"Yeah. Horace sends the post out when he can." Otto's jaw hardened at the mention of the storekeeper. "But we shouldn't expect an answer until spring, maybe even summer, given how slow things are. There are a couple people in town I could ask, too."

She nodded and worried her lip. Waiting didn't bother her, not when they had Trapper Dan's cozy cabin and the funds from selling the sheep. What had her gut churning was having to interact with that horrible Horace again. In the past when people treated her poorly, she'd hidden in her family's home, stewing behind the keys of her piano, but she couldn't do that here. She pushed back her shoulders. No, she was done hiding.

CHAPTER 26

Otto glanced down the street toward the store, wondering for the hundredth time if leaving Klara there alone to post her letter and shop was a smart idea. She'd insisted on confronting the cantankerous man on her own, and Otto understood the need to prove herself. Didn't mean he liked it.

He ducked into the marshal's office. The sooner he talked to the man about the property, the sooner he could get back to his wife. The marshal straightened from his desk and lazily scanned Otto over. The relaxed set of the man's shoulders either meant he had a handle on the rough town or he had an in with the wrong side of the law. Otto sure hoped it was the former.

"Morning, Marshal." Otto tipped his hat. "I'm Otto Lee, and I'm looking for some information I hope you could help me with."

"Otto Lee." The marshal drew out each syllable of Otto's name with a smile, causing Otto's muscles to tense. "So, you're the man who ran off with the young lady the

Müller's were helping. You put them in a mighty pickle, from the sounds of it."

"Is that what they say they were doing?" Otto clenched his fists. "I don't reckon beating a woman in broad daylight after months of starving her and who knows what else is considered helping. If I hadn't stepped in that morning, Klara would probably be dead."

"Figured there was another side of the tale." The marshal leaned back in his chair. "Those two are too slick for their story to stick. I'm wondering why you didn't come to me to press charges."

"Klara didn't want to. Doesn't want to even think about them again." Otto shrugged. "Besides, pressing charges would mean proving what they did and going through a trial. The wonderful townsfolk of Fryingpan Town have already shown they'll think the worst of my wife just because she's mute. The better form of justice is for us to live our lives as the Good Lord would have us do. In time, our happiness will be more punishment to the Müllers than anything the court system would have issued."

"I like the way you think, young man." The marshal's lips tipped up on one side. "Jack Smith at your service. What can I do for you?"

Otto's shoulders relaxed, and he eased into the chair opposite Jack. "My wife's father had purchased property before moving out here. Both he and Klara's mother passed on the trek over, and we just found the information in his journal he left to Klara."

"The Müllers have been here for a few months. How is your wife just finding this now?" The doubt in Jack's voice made Otto like the man even more.

Seemed like a man of the law shouldn't just believe everything a person said.

"Well, honestly, when Klara was with the Müllers, every moment was about survival. After we got hitched, the one satchel she had got shoved in the trunk. Between the healing and figuring out a new way of life, she just forgot about it."

Jack sat forward. "I can see that happening. Life gets mighty hard and hectic out here."

Otto nodded. No use chitchatting about it. Everyone knew life in the West wasn't easy.

"So, what property are we talking about?" Jack got down to business.

Otto opened the journal to the map and set it on the desk. "Alf Sorg bought this storefront here, plus another piece of land further outside of town. If I'm reading this right, it looks like the building next to the store."

"That's correct, all right." Jack huffed a laugh. "Horace was pretty miffed when he found out it'd been bought. When the Sorgs didn't arrive, I figured they'd either changed their minds or decided to wait until spring."

"Nope. They died a day into the mountains." Otto hated that Klara had to live through that. "Cholera."

Jack's face scrunched. "Well, that don't seem right. Haven't heard of cholera on the trail from Denver."

Cold settled into Otto's gut as the news turned over in his head. If not cholera, then what killed Klara's parents?

"Granted, we don't always hear about it, especially all the way out here. And it could've been something that looked like cholera. The journey west isn't a walk in the park." Jack tapped the journal. "Sorg was mighty particular about what he wanted. He insisted on a two-story since his family would live on the top floor while their house was built. The way he went on in the letters he sent, he planned on bringing a wagon full. Whatever happened to that?"

"Müllers took it and the stuff in it as payment for keeping Klara, even though they'd already been paid handsomely by her pa."

"That don't seem right."

"A lot of what happens out here doesn't."

"That's the truth." Jack shook his head. "I reckon Klara has a claim to both properties."

"We're thinking the same. She's posting a letter to her pa's old partner back home to see if there's a will somewhere."

"What will you do with it if it's hers?"

"Sell it, most likely." Otto shrugged. "We don't have much use for the one in town, and we could use that money to build our own place on the other property. Where we are now is temporary."

"Horace will jump at the chance to buy it."

Otto's lip curled at the mention of the storekeeper. "Know of anyone else who'd be interested?"

Jack burst out laughing. "What'd Horace do this time?"

"Let's just say him listening to the Müllers' lies and treating my wife like she wasn't only dumb but also a thief may have lost him the chance to expand the size of his store."

"That's the problem with these camp towns that pop up. People like Horace open shop. His demeanor's necessary when it comes to handling the rough characters these places draw, but, once families start moving in, people like him forget the decency that comes with family folk. This town is growing. He'll need to adjust before someone else sees an opportunity, pops a tent, and provides better."

"You don't mind keeping all this quiet, do you?" Otto stood, talking of Horace needled him to get back to Klara. "I'd rather not have it spread about town that we own these properties until we know for sure. Like you said, the men here are rough. I'd hate for anyone to jump the claim, so to speak."

"You have my word." Jack walked around the desk and extended his hand. "I have a contact at the land office in Denver I'll get a letter to. Maybe between Sorg's partner and my contact, we can get this sorted before spring, especially if I make it an official investigation."

He winked and clapped Otto on the shoulder.

"I appreciate that." He startled at the easily offered help.

"This town needs more honest, family-oriented people like you. The faster I can usher them in, the easier my job will be."

Jack's words filled Otto with a sense of hope and honor that he hadn't felt since he'd made one mistake after another and cost his family their lives. He didn't think he could ever see his way through the shame. If the marshal knew how reckless and stupid Otto had been in Leadville—if Jack knew that in a drunken revelry Otto had signed his pa's death sentence—honest and family-oriented would be the last words used to describe Otto.

He nodded to Jack and left. Otto needed to keep his head facing forward at his future, but his past kept clawing at his back. Whispered words denouncing who he now claimed to be tore at any thread of hope found. It was hard not to listen when they were filled with truth.

With a shake of his head, he jerked the door open. He couldn't wallow in pity, not when he had a wife who needed him. As he rushed onto the boardwalk, he plowed into a man.

"Watch it!"

The voice he hoped he'd never hear again slammed into his ears, snapping his gaze up. The men who'd killed his pa snarled at Otto. All feeling rushed from his head and swooshed out his toes. He stumbled back, his head spinning.

Recognition sparked in the leader of the murderous trio's eyes, and a sneer stretched slowly across his lips. "Well, now, if it isn't our gold mining pal."

The other two looked to the leader standing between them, then cocked their heads as they examined Otto. If his hands and feet weren't numb and his blood wasn't roaring in his ears, he'd find the matched confusion of the pair humorous.

"How's Lady Luck been to you lately?" The leader laughed, using Otto's own foolish words to taunt him.

Otto's eyes darted from one to the other, not knowing what to do. These men shot his pa in cold blood and stole their claim. Otto's hands twitched to gun them down right where they stood. Because of his cowardice and running instead of going to the authorities, these men would never see justice.

So why not be the hand that yielded it?

He flexed his fist next to his holster. With the stench of alcohol surrounding the three, Otto could get the drop on them. He'd avenge his pa and make right his mistake.

His gaze slid over them and snagged on Klara through the store window across the street. The sun haloed her golden hair as she read whatever she held in her hand. If he gave into the vengeance-demanding action, she'd be left alone to fend for herself again. If he didn't get killed in the process, he'd sure as shooting hang from the gallows. One couldn't gun down men in the streets, even if most of the buildings were canvas tents.

The door opened behind him, and Jack cleared his throat. "Problem?"

"No, sir." The leader tapped the brim of his hat. "Just bumped into each other is all." He winked at Otto. "See ya around, boy."

As they sauntered off with a laugh, Jack clapped Otto on the shoulder and went back inside. Otto kept his eye on their retreat as he crossed the street to the store. The man's parting wasn't friendly. No, to Otto that was a threat. Only this time, he'd be prepared.

CHAPTER 27

KLARA'S STOMACH turned as she stepped past the pickle barrel toward the sewing area. Horace's beady eyes watched her every move. Since there weren't but a few customers milling about, he didn't have any distractions to pull his attention away.

Oh, why hadn't she gone with Otto? Why had she insisted they split up? Sure, they'd get their errands finished quicker so they wouldn't be too late leading the flock back to the sheepfold, but that seemed like a poor excuse now that the horrible man stared at her like she was a thief.

She straightened her back even more and adjusted her basket hanging on her arm. If he had a problem with her, so be it. She wasn't a thief. Until there was another option, she'd give the vile man her business with a smile and quick thinking.

Skimming her fingers over the small selection of knitting needles, she picked the largest size available. Maybe it would be easier to learn with. She then chose a plain black yarn from the display. While she was getting better at spinning, it would be a while still before she produced a yarn worth making something out of. The black yarn wouldn't stain as easily as the lighter colors would if she happened to knit a garment that didn't require unraveling and starting over.

She sighed, half wishing they lived closer to town so that she could have lessons from Betty more than on Sunday afternoons. Trying to squeeze her domestic education into so few hours left her frustrated. Yet she also loved the isolation their homestead gave them.

A couple cowboys raced their horses down the street, whooping and hollering without caring who got in the way. Klara watched with her heart in her throat as they barely missed running over a hunched-over man crossing the street. She shook her head. No, she'd be happy with the occasional lesson in cooking, knitting, and sewing if it meant they could live away from the rowdiness.

As she turned to finish her shopping, her gaze snagged on Otto opening the door to the marshal's office. Oh, sugar peas. She needed to hurry up if she wanted to confront Horace the Heckler on her own.

A brown and orange can on the shelf snagged her attention, rushing her back to the past. She lifted the Baker's Breakfast Cocoa from the shelf and turned it over to read the instructions. She'd loved having hot chocolate in the morning when she'd lived in Ohio with her parents.

She'd sipped the sweet drink while her mother had fussed about all she had to do for the day and her father had read the paper while he ate breakfast. At the time, it'd been mundane. A daily occurrence not worth noting.

Now, though, she'd give anything to sit around the table with them.

She blinked away the moisture building in her eyes. Curling her fingers around the canister, she brought her hand to her chest. She'd been more prone to tears lately, and it needed to stop. Wallowing in the middle of the store would do no good. In fact, it'd set her back. She'd get the cocoa, make some when they got home, and let the memories, both good and painful, wash over her while she sipped it by the fire. But she would not cry in the dry goods aisle.

Decision made, she marched to the last item on the list, grumbling that the corner was so dark she could hardly read the labels. Otto had asked her to get more liniment, but the light was so bad, she couldn't tell if she was holding liniment or cough tincture. She twisted to get better lighting, smiling at the liniment label.

Without warning, a body shoved her into the shelf. The putrid smell that had haunted her for months filled her nose and made her gag. Hot, wet breath slid across her neck and into her ear.

"Miss me?" Hildebert's voice rasped, making her legs quake.

He ran his hands along her bodice, and her breakfast threatened to rush up her throat. She jerked and tried to free herself, but her trembling made the attempt weak. When he loosened his hold just enough for her to put an inch of space between them, his quiet laugh brought tears to her eyes.

"I love how you fight." He pushed his face into her hair and breathed deeply. "Makes me wish I had taken you when we first made it to this wretched town.

Foolish me, thinking wearing you down would be better."

She closed her eyes and clenched her jaw. He no longer had any power over her. She wasn't lost and alone anymore. Wasn't weak and starving. She could get away from him. She just had to move.

Move!

Stepping sideways on pudding legs, she swung her arm as hard as she could and slammed the liniment bottle into his groin. He wheezed a strange inward scream that held no weight and collapsed to the ground. Her breath bottled up in her chest, and black spots danced before her eyes. She couldn't just stand here. Taking a deep breath and carefully placing the bottle in her basket, she stepped around him and made her way to the counter. She smoothed her shaking fingers over her hair and pulled on her dress to make sure it was straight.

He might spread more rumors about her, but hopefully his sense of pride would keep him from admitting the "mute idiot" had taken him down. She honestly didn't care, one way or the other. She just wanted to get away from him.

As Horace tallied up her items, she focused on slowly taking deep breaths. Between the contrasting smells of the store and Hildebert's attack, her already queasy stomach threatened to revolt. She needed out of there. Needed the fresh air of the homestead that smelled of crisp water plants and drying grasses.

The bell over the door rang just as she handed Horace her money. Otto held her gaze as he stomped up to the counter. He glared at Horace, then took the basket from the counter.

"Ready?" Otto's voice held an urgency to it.

She nodded and threaded her hand through his offered arm. A low moan sounded right before Otto opened the door, but the bell covered the noise. She stifled a shudder and left without even looking Hildebert's way.

CHAPTER 28

OTTO'S FOREHEAD furrowed as he counted through the sheep for a fourth time that morning. How could five woolies be missing? He quickly scanned the flock, his heart pounding hard in his chest. When his gaze snagged on Baron, his breath whooshed out of him. His dog being uninjured left more questions tangling in his head.

Had the sheep wandered off together yesterday while they were grazing? He had gotten distracted by the mule deer during his evening count. Taking down the animal so they could have meat had been more important than getting an accurate tally. Besides, the sheep were always there.

Except, now they weren't.

He kneed Lemy toward the meadow the sheep had grazed at the day before without looking back at the cabin. Klara knew he planned on scouting more meadows further out while the snow was still lower than ankle deep. No use telling her he'd also be looking for lost sheep.

Whistling to Duke and Baron, he led the flock away from the homestead. His gaze scanned the ground for any sign of a group of sheep wandering off from the others. With there not being any new snow the night before, hopefully, signs of them would be easy to find. Though, since the last snow was a good ten days before, the woolies had trampled a lot of the area he'd had them graze.

He clenched his jaw, and pain spiked to his temples. Finding tracks in this mess would be next to impossible. Clicking his tongue for Lemy to pick up the pace, Otto pushed the sheep along faster. The sooner he could get them settled and grazing for the day, the sooner he could widen his search past the well-trodden path.

Once the sheep were happily munching away, Otto left both Duke and Baron to keep watch, much to Duke's dismay. Then, with a slow gait, Otto worked his way out from the flock and circled back toward the sheepfold. He kept the trodden meadow and path a rough fifty feet off and scanned the ground for hoof prints. By the time he got back to the sheepfold fencing, his neck ached and his impatience rose.

"Nothing," he growled, and Lemy's ears pricked up. "Well, Lem, let's work our way down the opposite side back to the sheep. Maybe the woolly monsters went off toward the creek."

Though the sheep veering through the woods to get to water made little sense because the meadow he'd had them grazing bordered the creek. But, as he'd discovered over the last year, sheep often lacked brains. With a quick prayer for patience and sight, he headed back toward the meadow on the opposite side of the path.

The creek gurgled just past the shrubs. The steady plod of Lemy's feet and the twittering of the birds as they flitted to and fro soothed some of Otto's annoyance. He needed to stop worrying about if he'd find the sheep and start looking at what he had in his favor.

First off, he had a Savior who forgave him and a beautiful, intelligent wife who loved him. Though, if Klara knew exactly what he'd done in his past, how he was responsible for all his family's deaths, that love might not be so readily given. He swallowed the lump in his throat that seemed determined to stick there ever since the run-in with his pa's murderers. He'd been on edge, vacillating between divulging all his worst secrets to Klara and keeping them buried with the dead. He hadn't come to a decision, and Klara had noticed his teetering mood.

He shook his head and continued his list. Secondly, the weather had been in their favor so far that winter. Despite it being December, the snow barely reached over the toes of his boots. The sheep could easily dig at the fluff and find the dead grass beneath. The lack of snow also made it easier to move them further from the cabin each day, so, if winter did eventually turn against them, there would still be meadows to graze from closer to home. He might have to shovel them out if it got deep, but at least he wouldn't have to travel far to do that.

The health of the flock thrived, much more than the winter before. The sheep were so healthy they apparently could wander away without a care in the world. Otto snorted, his spirits lifting enough to be slightly amused.

A snap up ahead whipped his gaze up and his sidearm out. He pulled Lemy to a stop and scanned the trees and brush. His pulse thudded in his ears, making it hard to hear. The loud snap could only have come from a good-sized animal. Was it another deer, the sheep, or something more predatory?

Lemy's ears twisted toward the left, and Otto searched that area. He'd have to rely on his horse's hearing since his own was overpowered by his hammering heart. Lemy's ears flicked again. Otto leaned over Lemy's neck, trying to see through the shrubs, but nothing was there. And if something was there, Otto sure as shooting couldn't see it.

A squirrel chattered angrily deeper in the woods. Otto sat back into the saddle. Whatever had been there seemed to have moved off.

Otto eased Lemy in the direction the horse's ears had pointed. Holding his pistol against his thigh, his eyes darted left and right, lingering on all the shadows before moving on. He scanned the tree branches looking for mountain lions. He'd heard too many stories of men being pounced on from above, and with the way his hair was standing up in warning, he wasn't taking any chances of being caught off guard.

Bright red smeared against the white snow and brown dirt visible through a gap in the brush to the left snagged his attention. He reined Lemy that way, keeping his eyes and ears open to the hibernating forest around him. The rattling of the bare branches and crisp cold suddenly didn't induce the peace it had just moments before.

When he got close, his heart sank at the sheep's mutilated body. Large mountain lion prints surrounded the carcass, leaving trails of red where the predator had walked. Otto shoved his pistol into his holster. The cat would be long gone by now.

Otto bowed his head and rubbed his hand over his

eyes. Great. Like he needed any more trouble. If the mountain lion decided it liked the taste of mutton, Otto could lose even more sheep before he took down the slick predator.

With a huff, he circled the dead animal looking for tracks. He tipped his head to the side. Something wasn't quite right. The cat had come in from the west, not the east where the flock was. He stared at the ground. There weren't any drag marks anywhere. It was like the ewe had been dropped there.

Circling the site in a wider arc, Otto's frustration mounted. There were so many big and small tracks scurrying about, he couldn't distinguish between any of them. Otto had a high suspicion it hadn't been an accident.

CHAPTER 29

WHILE KLARA WAITED for the water to boil so she could wash the laundry, she sat on the boulder next to the creek and drew in the journal Otto had bought her the Sunday before. She shaded in the lips on Otto's face, smiling at the memory of him tentatively giving her the journal. His mouth had curved up on one side as he'd explained the journal was for whatever she wanted it to be for, but not for communicating. That's how she drew him, with his nervousness twitching his lips and furrowing his brow, but his love for her sparking in his eyes.

She smoothed her fingers along the jawline to create more shadow there. Drawing, like music, had been another of her escapes growing up. Would Otto be surprised by yet another of her useless skills?

Mother had insisted Klara learned to paint, since doing so would make her more marketable. Of course, Mother had never said it like that. No, she'd use words like "socially acceptable hobby" or Klara's favorite, "Be beauty and create beauty."

SONG OF A DETERMINED HEART

Klara snorted a laugh at the memory. Then her throat closed with unexpected emotion. A tear dropped onto the drawing, and she quickly dabbed it away so it didn't spread. The spot still marred the shading on Otto's cheek, like he had been the one crying.

She closed the journal as more emotion overwhelmed her. Blinking to dispel the suddenly flowing tears didn't help. She hugged the journal to herself as sob after sob shook her body. Why was she even crying? Thinking of her mother had made Klara laugh, yet she just couldn't seem to stop the flowing emotion.

Was she even more broken than she had thought? Had something snapped in her? She felt like a cracked and crumbling dam with all its stored water pushing and breaking the fissure even more. She took deep breaths, wiped her eyes on her sleeve, tried to stand but failed, and everything she did made her cry even harder.

Her stomach turned. She was going to be sick. Tossing the journal onto the rock, she dashed for the creek and fell to her knees at the water's edge as she lost her breakfast. The sobs and retching ached her body, and frigid mud squished between her fingers.

Then, as quickly as she'd been overwhelmed, the episode passed. She watched the clear, icy-cold water pass over her fingers as she slowed her heaving breaths. Her heart still raced in her chest, but at least she could inhale and exhale slowly.

She rubbed her trembling hands together to get the mud off, then splashed the frigid water on her face. Taking another deep breath, she straightened her back and stared across the creek. The water meandered over the rocks and along the bank in an unwavering song.

Birds added their trilling as they flitted through the trees. The breeze tapped the branches together as nature's percussion. All of it soothed her until she felt herself again.

Not thinking about whatever had just happened was the best option. If she spent any time mulling over whether she was going insane or was simply a broken mess, she'd lose her composure. The last thing she needed was Otto finding her carrying on in the mud.

She pushed to her feet and cringed at her dress. Mud caked the front of the skirt. Her hair fell forward as she inspected her clothing, and she huffed out a frustrated breath. For the love of Pete. How had her hair gotten muddy? She couldn't remember touching it, but her blonde tresses now sported a lovely coating of brown.

Well, there was one way she could do both chores at once. She stomped to the fire where her washing pot of water rolled in an angry boil, snatched the soap bar from the tin box, and stomped back to the creek. She only hesitated long enough to kick off her boots. Then, arms swinging and legs stretching wide, she plunged forward.

When she got far enough from the bank that the water reached just over her knees, she took a deep breath and sat down. The shock of the frigid water covering her chest froze the air in her lungs. For a moment, they stopped working, and she tried not to panic. Then, her body relaxed, and she took a deep breath.

While the rush of water around her body was a welcome sensation, this was not a bath she'd want to linger in. She quickly dunked her head back, gasping as she came up. Gripping the soap tight so it wouldn't slip from her fingers and rush downstream, she attacked her hair.

Once it was all sudsy and rinsed, she scrubbed her skirt. It'd still have to go into the wash pot, but hopefully she could get the worst of it off. If nothing else, it'd keep the mud out of the pot and keep her from having to change the wash water more than once.

She shoved the soap in her pocket and let her hands skim the surface of the water. Now that her body had gotten used to the cold, she wanted to linger just a moment more. She closed her eyes and listened to the gurgling water, singing birds, and tapping breeze.

Yes, this life was hard, but she could do it. She had purpose and love, two things she never imagined having. For the first time in years, she felt herself.

Her body jerked in a shiver, and she laughed. It was probably time to get busy. Otto would really think her off her rocker if he came home and found her sitting in the creek.

As she stood, a branch snapped in the forest, breaking the peace. A squirrel yelled angrily. Another shiver rushed down her spine, but this time it wasn't from the cold.

Keeping her steps calm, she walked from the creek and grabbed her boots. As inconspicuously as she could, she scanned the surrounding trees and bushes for movement. There wasn't any, but then again, prey hardly ever saw the predator coming.

With goosebumps covering her skin and the sensation of eyes on her, she made her way to the cabin, snagging her journal as she passed the boulder. She reached the cabin and bolted the homemade lock, then she rushed to the window and checked that the shutters were still closed tight. She was probably being paranoid, thinking eyes were watching when they weren't, but she'd had that sensation before—living with Hildebert Müller.

CHAPTER 30

Otto's gaze scanned the buildings along the street as he stomped from the parsonage to the marshal's office. He'd left Klara visiting with Betty while he ran an errand. Guilt coated his throat like dust from a parched trail. Hiding his suspicions about the missing and killed sheep a secret from Klara was meant to keep her safe. So why did it leave him feeling ashamed?

Gritting his teeth so hard his temple throbbed, he marched to the marshal. He should just tell her. If he lost her trust and respect because of his foolish actions, he couldn't blame her. Not when what he'd done still curdled his stomach.

Even though he wasn't the weak man he'd been in Leadville. Even though he'd wised up and lived every day to be better. Even though he'd found forgiveness for the sins that destroyed his family at the base of the cross, he still lived with the consequences of loose lips and running away. If he'd gone to the law when the men had killed his father and jumped their claim instead of hightailing it out of there, the same men wouldn't be threatening Otto's family once again.

He wouldn't stay silent this time. He'd do whatever he had to in order to keep Klara safe, even if that meant he confessed his cowardice and part in Pa's murder. Surely knowing the story would show the marshal the true nature of the men.

Stopping in front of the office, Otto took a deep breath, scanned the street one last time, then opened the door with a determined jerk. Marshal Smith lounged with his feet on his desk, drinking coffee from a tin mug, and reading a paper. His head lazily lifted to peer at Otto, but his gaze had iron focus. He may give off the vibe of a laid-back man, but beneath the persona, a snake coiled.

Good.

Hopefully that focus would turn to the men after Otto finished laying everything out.

"Morning, Marshal." Otto tipped his hat and reached his hand across the desk.

Easy as could be, Marshal Smith sat up straight, set the paper he'd been reading upside down on the desk, and clasped Otto's hand. "I believe I told you to call me Jack."

He smiled, easing Otto's muscles even more.

"Sorry. Old habits." Otto took the seat across from Jack.

"You make a habit of being in the presence of the law?" Jack lifted one eyebrow, his shoulders tightening just a smidgen.

If Otto hadn't been watching, he'd have missed it.

"Oh, no." He laughed, rubbing his neck. "At least not in a bad way. Pa's friend back home was the sheriff. Even though he came for dinner every Thursday and I'd known him since birth, I still called him Sheriff Waters. Even Pa called him that when anyone else was around. Said wearing the badge was a hard and dangerous occupation that demanded our respect."

"I'd like to meet your pa. Maybe you could talk him into coming out to visit and teaching some of these boys his line of thinking." Jack leaned forward and pointed his chin toward the window.

The friendly suggestion dropped a boulder of grief in Otto's gut. His father had been a man of honor, and because of Otto, his life had been cut short. If Otto ever had children, he'd do everything he could to pass on his father's legacy and teachings. Hopefully, his children would listen better than he had.

"He's no longer with us." Otto clenched his hands around the hard wooden armrests of the chair.

"I'm sorry to hear that." Jack slumped back into his chair.

"That's part of the reason I'm here." The wood bit into his hand as he squeezed harder.

"Oh? How's that?"

"We've been having sheep disappear. While occasionally a predator will get an animal or a woolly will wander off and not be found, that's not what's happening."

"Rustlers?"

"Of a sort." Otto furrowed his eyebrows and inhaled out a bracing breath. "Three of the five sheep that went missing were slaughtered and placed where I would find them, and I believe I know who did it."

Jack's eyebrows rose and disappeared up under his cowboy hat. When he didn't talk, Otto filled the silence with a story he'd only told to two other people, Trapper

Dan and Orlando Thomas, the man who'd believed in him enough to give him a chance at sheep ranching. The telling was hard, but Jack's silence and nods of encouragement propelled Otto forward, leaving nothing out to absolve his own blame.

"These men are here and confronted you?" Jack asked when Otto slumped in his chair.

"Yes. They're the ones you interrupted when I came to talk about Klara's parents."

"I thought something was off about that situation." Jack leaned forward and put his elbows on his desk. "Why didn't you come to me then?"

"What could you do?" Otto scoffed. "Any evidence of them murdering my pa would be gone now."

"True, but I would've known to keep an eye out for them." He lifted an eyebrow in a preachy way, and Otto tried not to let it raise his hackles.

"I know." Otto huffed out his frustration with himself.

"I can come out and take a look around. Won't hurt to have another set of eyes look over the area." Jack shook his head. "Only problem is without evidence, my hands are tied."

Otto knew that, but knowing didn't lessen the disappointment.

"Know of anyone around here trustworthy enough to hire?"

"To shepherd?" Jack chuckled and shook his head. "You know as well as I do that most cowboys don't take to woolies."

Otto suppressed a groan and rubbed his neck. Cattle ranchers had been disparaging sheep ranchers for several years. If it kept up, the tensions might escalate to a full-on war.

"I can discreetly ask around though." Jack lifted one shoulder. "There might be a few who wouldn't mind now that's winter's coming on."

"I appreciate it." Otto stood. No use sticking around when Jack couldn't do anything.

"I'll ride home with you and check things out." Jack stood and stretched. "And if anything else happens, you be sure to tell me."

Otto nodded, though he didn't know if it would help. If he stayed with the flock, he left Klara unprotected. Yet, if he didn't guard the sheep, they could all be slaughtered while he slept.

Maybe he could convince her to stay in town with Pastor James and Betty? She'd be safe then. And if what happened to Otto's pa happened to him, she'd have someone to take care of her through the winter.

CHAPTER 31

Klara groaned as her eyes wandered from her father's journal to the empty cabin around her. The fire crackled in the hearth, and a slight wind rattled against the shutter, but it wasn't enough. She missed the huffs of Otto as he'd work a piece of leather or wood, whatever it was he tinkered on through the evening. She missed the heat his presence filled into the small space. Though she knew it was just her mind, the cabin felt colder without him there.

Duke whined at her feet, and she rubbed behind his ears. He understood her gloom. He'd been just as remorseful as she was since Otto left to guard the flock.

Klara's heart beat faster in her chest. When Otto had told her about the rustlers and that they were the same men who had killed his father, she had wanted to beg Otto to stay with her. Yet, the determination in his eyes and the need to prove himself in his voice held her back. So instead of begging him to stay, she'd firmly refused to be shuttled off to the James's, much to Otto's dismay. She refused to be hidden away, like her parents had done to her for so many years. If she and Otto were going to forge a life in the West, he'd have to trust that she could hold her own when they had to divide to conquer troubles.

She turned back to her reading. Just a few more pages remained in the journal. She'd savored the words her father had written, taking her time to read each entry several times before moving to the next. She'd wanted to gorge on it, inhaling the words so fast that she'd grow lightheaded from them. Somehow she'd known she'd regret not taking her time. She could only read the words for the first time once. Every time after reading it the first time might not be as special.

Flipping the page to the next entry, her breath caught at the date. It was the day before her parents died. Her father's handwriting was shaky, not like his normal tight and perfect penmanship. The vise tightening her throat almost made it hard to swallow.

I believe I may have made a mistake in trusting the Müllers.

Her father's opening sentence shook the remorse away as stark shock took root. Klara sat up straighter in the chair. Her eyes greedily raced over the shaky words.

My Emeline and I have both taken sick suddenly, and I can't believe the excuse of cholera dropping from Hildebert's lips when his eyes are full of greed and malice. He's poisoned us. I'm sure of it. But it will be hard to prove when we're both dead.

I have to warn Klara. Oh, what a fool I've been. She has to rely on the Müllers to get her to Fryingpan Town, but how do you trust the poisonous snake that's just struck a deadly blow? I need to somehow convince Hildebert it's in his best interest to keep Klara alive, even if it's just to get her to the town. Then she can take the strongbox hidden on the underside of the wagon beneath the bench and use the funds there to procure protection and passage home. Thank God I didn't tell Hildebert about it.

Klara stood, the journal dropping to the floor. There was a lock box of money in the wagon? Had the Müllers found it? She paced the small room, scanning her memories of when they'd arrived and all her family's possessions had been sold off.

She relived the heartache of unloading the precious items only to have to load them into someone else's wagon. Hildebert had been frustrated after the wagon had been cleared of its load, growling and shaking as he searched under the seat and beneath the bed. He'd been searching for the box. He must have been so confused when one wasn't found. He'd grumbled about the decent-sized sack of money found among her father's clothing not being enough.

Stopping her pacing, she stared at the shutters toward town like she could see the Müller's place if she stared long enough. If he never found the money, then that meant it was still hidden on the wagon. She closed her eyes, remembering her father pushing the journal into her hands and insisting she keep it hidden.

Keep it a secret.

She had to go get that money. Looking around the cabin, she rushed to her boots and yanked them on, pausing when her second foot was halfway in. She should wait for Otto. She really shouldn't go by herself. Biting her lip, she closed her eyes. What if the Müllers found it? Who knew how many nights Otto would have to stay with the sheep, and there was no way they could just walk up to the Müller's house during the day and start ripping the wagon apart?

Though Otto said Marshal Smith would help them, she didn't think he could help them with this. Hildebert could claim the wagon was his, and there was no way to disprove it.

Duke whined and touched his nose to her hand. She stared down at the dog. If she took him, she wouldn't be going alone. In fact, though he was more of a herding dog, he definitely was also a guard dog. That was why Otto had left Duke there with her.

Decision made, she pushed her foot the rest of the way into the boot and gathered what she'd need. Almost an hour later, she rode Lemy bareback toward the Müllers. Everything looked different in the dark, and she began to worry that she'd gone off course and missed it. She puffed out a frustrated breath and pulled her shoulders back. It didn't matter. If she missed it, she'd just end up in Fryingpan Town. From there, she could double back and find the house fairly easily.

She crested a hill and yanked Lemy to a stop. The house loomed before her, dark against the sliver of a moon. She'd been thankful for the small light, knowing if it was a full moon, she might not be able to do this. But now, she wished she had more light. The small crescent made the house appear ghostly, like it emerged from the pits of hell as a dark growth against the almost black sky.

She tied Lemy to a tree, keeping him hidden from the house, and rubbed his nose. "Stay here and keep quiet."

The darling snuffed into her hand and nodded. She would have laughed if nerves weren't skittering up her throat. Trekking a large circle around the house, she paused in the overgrown bushes behind the barn. The wagon was parked in its spot up against the back side of the barn, waiting for her twenty feet away.

Fear froze her muscles, and she wasn't sure if she'd be able to move. The expanse of space between the cover of the bushes and the wagon taunted her. She closed her eyes, swallowed the anxiety threatening to choke her, and willed herself to just go. Her body trembled. She couldn't do this.

She stifled a sound full of anguish and glared across the distance. Gripping her hand around the strap of her bag slung over her shoulder, she tried to push herself to go. Duke whined softly and placed his paw on her leg. Whether the action was in support or to push her forward, she wasn't sure. With a nod of resolution, she took it as the latter and crawled from her hiding spot.

Her frozen fingers hurt as they dug into the ground to help push her forward. Once out of the cover of the hibernating branches, she rushed across the crunching grass with Duke keeping right next to her. A door slammed when she was halfway there. Her heart exploded up her neck, pain ricocheting through her chest.

She wasn't going to make it.

Pushing her legs as fast as they could go, she sprinted across the grass. She barely heard the crunching of the grass beneath her feet and Duke's paws over the hammering of her pulse in her ears. She reached the wagon and dived underneath it, pulling Duke against her front, just as a dark shadow rounded the house.

Duke growled, and Klara shushed him. The form got

closer. Klara's entire body trembled, and her fingers went numb. She was surprised she could hold Duke to her body.

The shadow stopped in the middle of the yard. A strike of a match disrupted the silence of the night. Hildebert's face twisted into a sneer as he brought the match to his face and lit a cigarette. How could he look so antagonistic when there was no one but himself to terrorize?

He tossed the match to the ground, stomping on it with extra force. She tensed as his eyes scanned the dark. Even though the glow from the cigarette didn't light his face completely, she could tell he was searching.

Please. Please, Lord.

That was all she could pray as she stared wide-eyed at her captor and the man who most likely murdered her father. No other words of prayer came as she waited for him to see her.

Slowly, he meandered toward her hiding spot. She wasn't sure if it was better that she could no longer see his face or not. Duke's body rumbled next to her, and she placed a hand on his snout to quiet him.

A slow inhale and paper burning filled the air. The acrid smell rolled her stomach. She could almost feel Hildebert's sticky breath on her neck. He took another drag, then cursed low when a breeze tugged on his shirt.

"Stupid mountains and its stupid cold." He threw the cigarette to the ground right in front of her. "We should've headed back east the moment we got rid of the haul."

His foot ground the cigarette into the dirt before he spun and rushed back to the house. She'd never been more happy for the frigid wind as she was at that moment. Her muscles collapsed her fully to the ground, and she closed her eyes in relief. Hopefully, the foul man wouldn't come back out again.

She crawled to the front of the wagon, making sure to keep her head down so she didn't knock herself out on the wood and metal above her. That would be just her luck to have the Müllers find her unconscious in the morning.

When she got under the seat, she pulled the bag up and dug out a match and candle. She cringed at the brightness illuminating the space beneath the wagon. Hildebert might still look out the window, so she'd better make this quick.

She searched the wood for some sign or clue, but frustration mounted when she couldn't find anything. Shifting her angle, she ran her free hand over the wood. She gasped when she felt a familiar indention and quickly held the candle to the area.

Her family crest had been stamped into the wood at a spot that would be virtually unnoticeable. She surveyed the area around the crest, her face mere inches from the wood. A fine line circled the crest. Joy rushed through her when she realized what her father had done.

She twisted the crest to the left forty-five degrees, then to the right ninety degrees, and pressed. Just like the hidden compartment in her father's study back home, a slab of wood popped open. Tears streamed down her face as she pulled not one but three bulging sacks from the space. Not caring if she got caught, she peeked in the first and gasped at the gold filling it.

With a shaky prayer of thanks, she snuffed out the

candle. After three trips to carry the heavy sacks to Lemy, she tied the bags together and draped them across the horse's back. Her cheeks hurt from smiling as she swung herself up behind the bags. With a gleefulness that bordered on maniacal, she clicked for Lemy to take them home.

CHAPTER 32

OTTO SHIFTED ON THE COLD, unrelenting ground, trying hard to keep his mind from the warm bed and soft curves of his wife. Everything in him screamed to return home to her. It didn't feel right leaving her unprotected.

"Stop," he harshly whispered to himself for the hundredth time.

She wasn't alone. Duke would keep her safe, and she knew how to use the gun Otto had left. The cabin wasn't a flimsy tent like the one he'd shared with his father. Whoever had built Trapper Dan's home had done so with massive logs and a solid door. Klara would be safe within their protective walls.

A breeze blew across his neck, knocking the bare branches together above him. The chill slid down his coat. He shivered and pulled his collar and scarf tighter against him. His finger slipped through a space in the scarf, making him smile.

Klara had worked so hard on trying to knit him the scarf. He closed his eyes and pictured her before the fire.

Her bottom lip had pulled between her teeth as she'd concentrated on getting the stitches right. When she'd held up the knitted length to measure it, the crooked edges and sporadic holes had her eyes tearing in frustration. It had taken him wrapping the length around his neck and coaxing her out of her mood with promises that the scarf would keep him warm and soft kisses of thanks before she'd agreed her first attempt was passable.

Otto opened his eyes to the dark meadow before him. The sheep moaned and shifted in their sleep. An owl hooted as its wings beat behind him. Dried grass tapped and shuddered in the breeze. Other than that, silence blanketed the night.

Why was he even out there? He knocked the back of his head against the cottonwood with a growl. Did he plan on spending every night with the sheep? Imagining all manner of things happening and leaving Klara alone? No, his worry and focus were so divided, doing this night after night would likely kill him—a slow and torturous death. If he moved the sheepfold closer to the cabin, could he hear both the dogs and the sheep if something happened? Probably. He could stay with Klara and protect her and still be close enough to the sheep to stop any predators, four-legged or two.

Nodding, he huddled further into his coat. Tomorrow he'd move the sheepfold, even if it took all day. He wasn't spending another night away from Klara.

Otto scanned the tops of the sheep's backs, letting his gaze skim the brush on the opposite side of the clearing. A shadow shifted in his peripheral. Goosebumps crawled along his skin, standing his hair on end as he focused on the dark spot within the sagebrush. His pulse pounded in his ears, drowning out all other sounds. Gritting his teeth, he slowly inhaled and willed his heart to slow down.

He didn't move anything but his eyes as he searched the shadows. The sheep on the far side of the fold shifted. The rumble of Baron's growl filled the quiet better than any other warning. Otto's eyes hadn't deceived him.

Something was out there.

And if it was who Otto thought, he was outnumbered. His eyes traveled the perimeter of the clearing. Would the men have split up? Should Otto make his way around through the trees, hoping to come across the threat before they saw him? Or would it be better to tuck himself into the fold with the sheep and let their numbers hide him?

He glanced up at the sky, thanking God for the thin sliver of moon that would keep him more hidden either way. Though he supposed it also kept the attackers hidden, as well.

Sheep?

Trees?

Which would be better?

With a huff, he crawled from his post and melted into the trees. While hiding within the woolly beasts would give him an advantage, if the enemy attacked, Otto didn't want to have to push against the frenzied animals to engage the threat. He slinked through the woods, keeping his revolvers ready and his senses open. These men may have gotten the drop on him before, but he'd grown up since last they met.

The Rocky Mountains were a challenging teacher, demanding strength and wisdom to survive. Through hardship and grief, he'd learned his lesson. He'd do anything to keep his family—his Klara—safe.

Baron's white shape dashed from the sheepfold into the woods, and Otto froze. Cocking his head, he listened for any clue. Baron's menacing snarl twisted Otto's gut, snapping his attention to the sound. He wanted to rush to Baron's side to protect his faithful companion, but that might play right into the murderers' plans. Otto held to the shadows, shifting through the shapes of the forest as the sheep bleated warnings to each other that all was not right.

His palms slicked against the grain of his revolvers' handles. He swallowed the fear threatening to suffocate him. Movement across the clearing snagged his attention, and he adjusted to confront it. A mountain lion dashed from the cover of the sage and raced across the open grass. Baron chased, snapping at the cat's tail and barking.

The stress of the moment rushed from Otto, and he slumped against the tree next to him. He bowed his head and closed his eyes as his body shook from adrenaline. While it wasn't normal mountain lion behavior to come to a flock like that, he must've been the one that had found the carcass and wanted more.

Otto jammed his guns into their holsters and slid to the ground, hanging his spinning head between his knees. Tension coiled him too tight. He needed to get through this night, and then tomorrow he'd move the sheep closer to the cabin. If being in the cabin with Klara meant more sheep disappeared, so be it. Klara meant more to him than anything else. Keeping her safe was his priority, even if that meant losing the sheep. Together, they'd figure out another means of life.

He pushed up to his feet, keeping his weight against the tree for support. He exhaled his resolve to remain away the rest of the night and inhaled the peace he felt deciding to return to Klara. Tomorrow, they'd do what they could to make the sheep safer, but tonight ,he wasn't leaving her alone any longer.

Turning his attention and steps toward home, his eyes widened as fear cascaded down his spine, freezing him where he stood. A warm glow danced in the distance beyond the brush as smoke twisted into the sky.

Fire.

Klara!

CHAPTER 33

KLARA'S FACE HURT, more from smiling than the frigid wind. She couldn't believe she'd snatched back what was rightfully hers. She wanted to dance under the stars. To pound the ivory keys until the world rejoiced with her.

No.

What she really wanted to do was track down that husband of hers and kiss him senseless, maybe lie with him in the sliver of the moon and keep each other warm. Her cheeks heated, and she ducked her head.

How scandalous.

Her mother would've been horrified. Klara snickered at the thought of any of her past acquaintances doing something as wild as embracing their husband within the forest. Well, she no longer cared what that society thought of her. There was no one around for miles, and if she wanted to seduce her husband to abandon his post for her, why shouldn't she?

She squared her shoulders and lifted her chin high.

Celebration was in order. She didn't care if he got upset with her for searching him out.

Duke's growl just ahead of Lemy jerked Klara out of her musings. Not paying attention to the wilderness around her and getting attacked by some predator would definitely get in the way of her celebrating. Plus, Otto would be extra upset then.

She pulled Lemy to a stop and strained to hear what had Lemy's ears twitching forward and Duke baring his teeth. Raucous laughter and thundering hoofbeats had her breath hitching. She jumped from Lemy's back and pulled him into the thick brush. She whistled softly for Duke, snapping her fingers and pointing for him to sit at her side when he continued to growl and stand in front of her.

"Hush," she whispered just as three men on horseback emerged from the bend in the trail.

They didn't bother hiding. The torches they carried lit their sinister faces like it was broad daylight. Torches? She shook her head as they drew closer.

"We crushed him good, huh Davey?"

Snorts of glee filled the air, stabbing Klara's gut. Otto! She twisted her shaking hands into Lemy's mane.

"Definitely gave the fool a good blow, but that was just an appetizer, Mark. Tomorrow night we'll not only crush him. We destroy him, nice and slowly." The man in the middle sneered.

"Can't wait." Mark's excitement pushed vomit up Klara's throat.

The third man nodded, his stony face even more terrifying than the other two's exuberance. They kicked their horses into a gallop. The earth shook beneath her feet as they rumbled past.

She didn't wait for their retreat to fade but swung onto Lemy's back and urged him into a run. Her breath hitched in her chest so quickly that her head swam. She tried to calm herself, but the fear of finding Otto dead made that impossible. Bright orange lit the sky above the cottonwoods, and smoke tinged the air.

"Klara! No!" Otto's anguished roar sounded over the cracks and snaps of fire as she burst from the trees.

Flames consumed the cabin, reaching from the top of the roof into the night sky. She yanked on the reins so hard that Lemy reared, dumping her onto the dirt before he jolted away from the fire. The reins jerked from her hand, wrenching her arm.

"Klara!" Otto's cry tore her wide gaze from the blazing roof to where he slammed a large rock against the door.

"Otto!" Her scream wasn't louder than a whisper.

She scrambled to her feet as he rammed his shoulder to the burning door. The roof shifted and shuddered. It was going to collapse on him. She sprinted toward him, whistling and clapping to get his attention. Duke joined in frenzied barking.

Otto whipped around, his eyes on his soot-covered face widening. Just as he darted to her, the roof imploded with a horrifying whoosh, sending Otto to his knees. Klara's silent scream ripped from her lungs as the wall buckled and fell toward him. He scrambled away, a yell of pain splitting the air as a log landed on him.

Klara skidded to a stop beside him and tried to pull him out from under the rubble. Sobs heaved her chest when he didn't budge. Another wall crashed, shooting flames over their heads.

"Klara, go. Get to safety." Otto pushed her away.

She shook her head at the foolish man.

There was no way she'd leave him.

Ever.

She crawled to the log, put her hands on the burning wood, and lifted. Her muscles strained against the weight and fire scorched her skin, but she didn't dare let go. Praying for the strength of Samson, she gritted her teeth and pushed up with all her might. The log lifted, but not enough. Gulping down her whimper, she strained harder. The log inched higher, and with a howl, Otto yanked his legs from beneath.

He wrapped his arms around her and pulled her away. All her muscles collapsed like the burning walls before them. Otto kept dragging them backward away from the inferno. Her vision blurred, and darkness and pain threatened to pull her under. She didn't have the strength to fight anymore.

CHAPTER 34

Otto trembled, more from fear than the cold of the water. Klara's limp body floated in front of him, her head rolling against his shoulder. He knelt in the frigid creek and cradled her against him.

"Klara?" He brushed her pale hair off her even whiter cheek. "Klara, sugar, wake up."

Tears choked him, cracking his voice. He didn't know how she'd escaped the cabin. He wouldn't have stopped trying to get to her, to free her from the fiery death, even if it meant perishing himself. There was no way he could lose her and continue living.

He touched her cheek, then a burn on her neck, and finally her charred hands. His own blistered fingers shook with terror. Tears dripped into the creek, but his gut hardened in rage. Those men had nailed the door so tightly, Otto never would have been able to get to Klara. Had they thought he was in there as well? He needed to get Klara to safety, get the doctor, and then hunt down the monsters who would seal an innocent woman to burn alive. If the law wouldn't bring justice, Otto would. No matter the cost.

Klara's eyelids fluttered, and her teeth chattered. Her confused gaze met his, her forehead furrowing. Slowly, she lifted her hand and trailed her fingers along his cheek.

"Okay?" she mouthed.

He gently cupped his hand against hers and leaned his cheek into her palm. "Yes."

Staring down at her in the thin moonlight, his chest heaved, and a sob ripped from him. "I thought I'd lost you."

She shook her head, curling into him as a shiver assaulted her body. Duke whined from the shore, and another relieved breath whooshed from Otto. The Lord must have sent Klara and Duke outside at just the right time. Otto would thank Him every day of Otto's life for that providence.

"I have to get you to the doctor," Otto rasped, his throat raw from screaming and the smoke.

He went to stand, and pain shot up his calf. His knees buckled. Clinging Klara to him with one hand, he caught himself with the other before they both submerged completely.

A crash thundered over the roar of the fire, snapping his head up just in time to see the chimney and back wall slam into Lemy's stall. Otto tried to stand again, but his leg wouldn't stand. He had to get to Lemy. Had to save him.

"Lemy," Otto gasped as the stall erupted into flames.

"He ran," Klara's faint whisper barely reached Otto's ears over the roar of the inferno.

He looked down at her, his mind scrambling with confusion. "What?"

She pulled herself up so her mouth was right against his ear. "Lemy ran. Fire scared him."

Otto stared at his wife for several seconds as he tried to work out what had happened. Somehow, she had not only been out of the cabin but had also taken Lemy and Duke. She could tell him what had happened later. He needed to get her, and himself, to the doctor.

He waved a command at Duke. "Fetch Lemy."

The dog shot into the dark with a bark. When Otto shuffled to get his feet beneath him, Klara wiggled out of his arms. He didn't want to let her go, but his leg wouldn't allow him to stand and carry her. He prayed it wasn't broken. She wrapped her arm around his back, and together they stood. A sharp stab in his calf had him gritting his teeth so hard they'd crack, but he didn't lean on Klara more than necessary.

As they stumbled out of the creek, his horse trotted up with his reins dragging the ground and sacks slung over his back. Otto shook his head and pushed his hand through his hair.

"I think you've got some explaining to do, wife."

She looked from Lemy to Otto, tears swimming in her eyes. She gave a quick nod, then adjusted her arms around his back to support him more. He didn't miss the way she flinched when her hand brushed his or the way she held him with only her forearms.

When they emerged onto dry ground, he grabbed the reins and led Lemy to the jumble of boulders. Otto only grumbled a little as he used the stones to boost him up like a child. Mostly because he fought to not lose his stomach contents or pass out from the agony lifting his leg over Lemy's back caused. He took a deep breath to clear his vision, scooted back so Klara would have space in front of him, and reached his hand down. Her mount was just as ungraceful as his own, but she pressed her back into his chest with a sigh.

He wrapped one arm tight around her waist and whispered in her ear, "I was so scared I'd lost you, too."

As Lemy trotted past the burning remains of their home, Otto buried his face in Klara's neck. He fought to control his tears, but his body couldn't hold in his shudder. She leaned sideways and kissed his forehead.

"Me, too." She pressed her lips to his cheek. "I love you."

She captured his lips with hers, a desperation in her that mirrored his own. He lifted his hand to cup her cheek as he deepened the kiss only to hiss as blisters burst when he flexed his fingers in her hair. Her breath shuddered against his mouth as she touched his lips tenderly one more time before she tucked herself under his chin.

As they plodded toward town, both too injured to go any faster, she told him of her father's journal and the bags of gold hanging before her. His heart almost galloped away at the risk she'd taken going by herself, but if she hadn't, she'd be encased in a fiery grave.

Him with her.

Determination for justice flared with the thought of what could've happened. He clicked Lemy into a quicker pace. Otto needed to get Klara to the parsonage where she'd be safe, fetch the doctor, and then hunt him up some murderous polecats.

CHAPTER 35

KLARA SWALLOWED her whimper as Dr. Jones cleaned the burns on her palms. Betty stood at her kitchen counter, her shoulders stiff as she beat the flapjack batter in her bowl. Pastor James paced the length of the small kitchen, occasionally peeking out the window to check for Lord knew what. It wasn't like those men knew Klara and Otto were here. Marshal Smith stared at her from his chair across the table.

"You clearly saw their faces? Enough that you could point them out?" His jaw tightened, flexing his cheek.

She nodded. "Can draw them." Her voice was even raspier than normal. She glanced at her heavily bandaged right hand. "Maybe."

His eyes softened. "That won't be necessary, ma'am." His expression hardened again as he turned to Otto. "And you think these are the same men that killed your pa?"

Klara jerked her gaze to her husband. He knew the men that had murdered his father were in town and kept it from her? Why hadn't he told her?

"Yeah. Who else could it be?" He stared at his blistered hands and Klara's chest cinched as he struggled to control his emotions. "They nailed the door closed, Jack." Otto's voice cracked. "From what Klara overheard them say, they knew I wasn't in there, that I was out watching the flock. They meant to kill an innocent woman for what? To torture me before killing me, too? It's more than just greed. It's evil."

"'Forwardness is in his heart, he deviseth mischief continually; he soweth discord.'" Pastor James stopped pacing and rolled his shoulders back. "'Therefore shall his calamity come suddenly; suddenly shall he be broken without remedy.'"

"Amen to that." Betty slammed the bowl onto the counter and spooned her batter on a griddle with such malice Klara's lips tweaked.

"Amen, indeed." Marshal Smith pushed back his seat and stood. "After you came to me the other day, I scouted them out, but without any evidence to arrest them on, I couldn't bring them in. I know where they're staying and have men I trust to help me bring them in. I'll have them in custody within the hour."

"I'll come—" Otto went to rise but cringed when his leg hit the ground.

Marshal Smith held up his hand. "You're in no condition to join me."

Otto growled. "It's not busted. I'll be fine."

"Friend, stay with your wife. Let Doc patch you up and get some sleep." Marshal Smith put his hand on Otto's shoulder, and Klara's eyes teared up at the sign of camaraderie. "I have a feeling you aren't the only victims these men have had. With you and your wife's help, I'm going to make sure they get the justice they deserve. This town might be nothing but a pack of down-on-their-luck miners, but they won't take nicely to what those men tried to do to Klara."

Otto slumped in his chair with a nod. Klara slid her bandaged hand along his arm and patted his wrist. Otto would've pushed through the pain to take their enemy down, but she was glad he had others he could trust with that burden.

Marshal Smith turned his penetrating eyes to Klara, and she straightened. "Ma'am, after Otto came and talked to me about your pa's properties and how they passed, I started digging. The way they died didn't sit right with me."

She signed, "Why?"

Otto translated before she even realized her mistake. She'd been letting her hands talk more and more with Otto's encouragement.

"Well, we haven't had an issue with cholera in that area for years." Marshal Smith shook his head. "In my digging, I struck gold, so to speak. I found a poster with the Müllers on it. They're wanted for larceny, murder, and a long list of other crimes."

Betty gasped. "Dear Lord above."

Klara's chest tightened, and she leaned into Otto.

"I was going to bring them in tomorrow, but I can wait a few days if you want to be there."

"What if they get away?" Otto asked.

"The pass already closed up with snow. They won't be going anywhere anytime soon." Marshal Smith shrugged and shifted on his feet. "Now, you can't be right close when I arrest them, but I reckon if you stay on the property's edge until they are in custody, your presence won't cause any harm. I was thinking you could then go through the place and see if any of your family's belongings are still around. I'm not sure what all they got rid of, but there might be something of worth there."

Klara nodded as tears filled her eyes. She couldn't care less about worth. Just the thought of holding something of her parents' again was treasure enough.

"Well, one criminal gang at a time. I'll let you know when I have the men from tonight behind bars." He touched the brim of his hat and stomped determinedly out of the house.

Pastor James slid into the chair the marshal had vacated as the front door clicked shut. "This evening is stacking up to be one of many surprises."

And he didn't know about the gold. Klara blew out a tired breath.

"All done, dearie." Dr. Jones patted her hand. "Now, son, your turn."

Otto nodded with a sigh.

"You two are welcome to stay here as long as you need." Pastor James leaned back in his chair.

"Well, of course they are." Betty flipped the flapjacks with a *tsk*.

"You don't have any spare rooms." Otto shook his head.

"Pish posh." Betty wrapped her apron around her hand and lifted the percolating coffeepot off the stovetop, filling the mugs she'd lined up on the counter. "We'll just set up a spot for you in the living room. We both come from large families and know lots of ways to find space for more people."

Klara's heart swelled at Betty's easy offer. While the couple's house had an actual bedroom, the space wasn't much bigger than their own cabin had been. The thought of the cabin by the creek pricked, popping the swell like a bubble. Grief made the joy of friendship bittersweet. The fire had taken everything.

No.

Klara sat up straighter and gazed at her husband. The fire had only taken things. It hadn't taken what was most important. Otto would recover from his injuries the same as she would. They had the sheep and the properties her parents had purchased. They had the funds from the sale of the sheep hidden in the tree and the gold in the sacks tucked under Otto's chair. They'd rebuild Trapper Dan's cabin, then they'd build one of their own. And if they didn't want to stay there in the Roaring Fork Valley, they had the money to choose a different life…together.

"We appreciate the offer, especially for tonight, but we won't inconvenience you long." Otto hissed as Dr. Jones poured antiseptic over his burns.

Klara cringed, just having gone through the pain herself. Betty set a steaming mug in front of Klara, but she couldn't bring herself to drink it. She'd had enough heat for one night.

"Seriously. Winter's here, my friend." Pastor James smiled up at Betty as she handed him a mug. "We'd be happy to have you."

"Thank you. Your friendship means a lot to me." Otto cleared his throat and looked at Klara. "To both of us."

Klara blinked the tears away as she stared into her husband's loving eyes.

"We have options, though, so we won't have to put you

out for too long." Otto smiled and shrugged one shoulder. "Looks like Fryingpan Town will be getting two new residents, at least for the winter."

Betty clapped her hands. "Oh, I can't tell you how excited I am."

As Betty listed all the things she'd been dying to have a friend to do with, Klara laughed. That night had held so many twists and turns her head swam. Had it only been hours and not days since she'd read her father's journal entry? As Betty rattled on and Pastor James excused himself to set up a pallet for them to sleep on, Klara leaned into Otto's side, resting her head on his shoulder. It might take her days to come to terms with everything that had happened, but one thing was certain—God had redeemed her life more abundantly than she'd ever imagined possible.

CHAPTER 36

Klara leaned against Otto as a brisk breeze pulled at her skirt. They stood at the Müllers' property edge slightly hidden among the cottonwoods in the same place she'd built her courage a few nights earlier. She cocked her head, a smile playing on her lips. The wagon parked against the back of the barn looked closer in the daylight.

As Marshal Smith and his deputy sauntered up to the porch like they didn't have a care in the world, her heart threatened to pound out of her chest. What if something went wrong, and the Müllers took another innocent man's life? She didn't want to watch, but she couldn't pull her eyes away.

The marshal's knocking on the front door shattered the quiet morning's peaceful facade. The seconds stretched for days, causing her palms to sweat in the bandages. How in the world did these men do this day after day? The stress was about to explode out of her, whether by heart rupture or casting out her breakfast. She couldn't be sure, but it wouldn't be pretty.

Marshal Smith tipped his hat, then pointed toward town. His low murmured words didn't reach Klara, but she tried not to be offended by the seemingly pleasant demeanor of the marshal. Even though he'd told them his plan of luring the Müllers outside before they could barricade themselves in the house, Klara worried the ploy wouldn't work. These two had conned her father, one of the smartest men she knew. They wouldn't be duped by niceties.

Klara's jaw dropped as Maude sashayed out of the house, her hips swaying and fingers twirling her hair. Even across the yard, Klara could see Maude's eyelashes fluttering at Marshal Smith like autumn leaves flapping in the wind.

Dear Lord, did the woman have no decency whatsoever? Sure, the marshal was handsome, but Maude was a married woman. She stepped closer to Marshal Smith and ran her hand down his arm, letting out a falsetto laugh that sent shivers down Klara's spine. The laugh morphed into a shriek as the marshal slapped handcuffs on Maude's wrist.

"How dare you! Unhand me now." As she twisted to get loose, the wind blew and whipped her skirt in a loud snap behind her. "Hildebert! Help, Hildebert!"

"Keep shrieking...gag you." Marshal Smith's low, steady voice could barely be heard over the ruckus Maude made. He handed her to his deputy. "Gag her, tie her to the porch post, then follow me in."

Marshal Smith unholstered his revolver and stood off to the side of the front door. Maude let out a screech so high and loud that Klara was surprised the glass didn't shatter. It left Klara's ears ringing, and she almost missed the faint scraping coming from the barn behind the wagon.

She couldn't tear her eyes from the marshal as he peeked into the house, but she couldn't ignore the odd, low noise. More than likely, it was the wind pulling on the shabby barn wall. She bent to look below the wagon just to make sure.

A shout yanked her attention to the deputy stumbling after Maude, who was running away from the porch. Otto handed her his crutch and limp-dashed across the yard to help. Klara cringed, hoping he didn't injure his leg worse. Just as Otto tackled Maude to the ground, Hildebert jumped up from behind the wagon and took off toward the trees—directly toward Klara.

Her heart leaped right up into her throat at the same time Hildebert noticed someone was in front of him. His eyes widened, and his arms flailed as he attempted to change course. *Lord, help me.* Klara gripped the crutch and swung as hard as she could. The crack of wood on his skull spiked searing pain through her burned hands and vibrated up her arms almost causing her to drop the crutch. Hildebert dropped to his knees, one hand holding him up and the other covering the side of his head as he shook it. She tightened her hold and swung the crutch back, just in case she needed to hit him harder.

"Klara!" Otto scrambled to his feet and hobbled toward her, pain creasing his forehead with each step.

Marshal Smith leaped over the porch railing and sprinted across the yard. Hildebert groaned as the marshal pulled both hands behind his back and clicked the manacles into place. Marshal Smith yanked Hildebert to his feet. He stumbled, then shook his head to clear it.

His confused gaze hit Klara and cleared. "You."

Though Klara's stomach twisted at the sight of the man who had killed her parents and assaulted her, she shrugged and swung the crutch up so it rested on her shoulder. Hopefully, the man couldn't see how it trembled.

"Klara." Otto pulled her into his arms and brushed her hair that had fallen from her braid off her face. "Are you okay?"

She nodded, tossed the crutch down, and tucked her face into his neck. The ordeal was done, and her parents would get justice. She let out a shuddering breath as a tear broke free.

"We're going to go ahead and take these two into the jail." Marshal Smith motioned his chin toward the house. "Take your time going through the house. I want to make sure you get your family's things back. If you're not here when I'm done with these yahoos, I'll swing by the parsonage to get a recording of what you find."

Otto's Adam's apple bobbed against her cheek. "Thank you, Jack."

"No, thank you. Both of you. Without your help, these two would still be free." Marshal Smith cleared his throat. "Come on, Müller. I've got a nice, hard cot for you to wait your trial on."

Their footsteps crunched their retreat through the dead grass. She kept her face against her husband's neck. She didn't want to look at the two people who had taken so much from her ever again. Otto seemed to know what she needed, because he held her, rubbing a gentle hand up and down her back until the clop of horses' hooves disappeared into the distance.

"Ready, sugar?" He squeezed her closer.

She shook her head but pushed back from his embrace. With a fortifying inhale of crisp mountain air, she stepped toward the house. Horrible memories crashed over her as she walked through the door. So much pain and heartache rushed her that she almost backed out the door. She squared her shoulders and moved through the house.

She scanned the living room and kitchen as she passed toward the bedroom, not expecting to see anything of hers. The only thing she'd ever seen in the house of her family's was her mother's teacup. She now understood that the Müllers kept their shabby furniture instead of the items her parents had brought because of the price they could get for the quality pieces. Maybe they wouldn't have sold so much off if they'd realized they'd be stuck in Fryingpan Town for the winter.

Swallowing the lump in her throat, she stepped into the only bedroom. It was just as skimpily furnished as the rest of the house. It was a fool's errand coming there and expecting hidden treasure. Of course, the Müllers wouldn't want to keep any evidence of their crimes. She leaned back into Otto's secure arms with a sigh.

"Nothing?" His whisper rumbled in her ear.

She shook her head.

"Let's check the drawers just in case." He eased her away from him and went to the side table next to the bed.

She trudged to the dresser. When she pulled open the top drawer, her mouth fell open as her muscles froze. Her mother's pearl-backed brush lay nestled on top of cotton clothing. Her fingers trembled as she picked it up and hugged it to her chest. Her chin shook, and her vision blurred.

As a sob ripped from her chest, she one-handedly threw the clothing out on the floor. She grabbed a stocking to toss it with the rest when the weight of it stopped her. Otto stepped up next to her, and she handed it to him. He tipped the end into his hand. Her father's gold pocket watch he'd received on his wedding day from his father tumbled out.

Surprise and relief collapsed her legs, and she sat on the floor as her body shook with grief anew. Otto eased down beside her, not able to hide the hiss of pain in his leg. His eyes were glassy with unshed tears, and he gave her a sad smile. It didn't matter if they found anything else. She'd recovered treasures once cherished and found unbound blessings of love and respect in these Colorado mountains.

CHAPTER 37

Otto's boots beat a fast clip along the slick boardwalk as he came back from checking the flock. They'd moved them to Klara's family's property since it was closer to town and hired some men to help Duke and Baron keep an eye on the woolly beasts when Otto wasn't around. He shivered as a gust of wind sent a cascade of snow down his collar. He couldn't wait to get home and wrap his hands around a hot mug of coffee. Better yet, his wife was particularly good at heating him up. He picked up his pace, and his lips twitched up. Any faster and he'd be running.

Horace stood in the window of his store, scowling at the snow. Otto jauntily saluted the cranky man, causing him to scowl even more. Since Otto and Klara had moved into the storefront her father had purchased for his office, the storeowner had been even more mulish. Otto rolled his eyes as he passed the store. If Horace would just show some sign of civility, Otto and Klara would consider selling the town property to him once their cabin was built next summer. They had no desire or need to keep it, though maybe leasing the space would be a better option financially than selling it outright.

Otto froze with his hand outstretched toward the door handle. Life had truly changed. He'd lost everything—his family, their home, everything his pa and he had packed with them in their search for a new life. But through God's grace and the willingness of others to extend that grace, Otto found a hope and life he never imagined possible.

He inhaled the crisp clean air the snow brought with it and pushed into his home.

His future.

Klara stood at the table they'd been given by one of the saloon owners. All their scant furniture had been donated by others, just another proof of the Lord's mercy and provision. Flour covered her cheeks and apron. Her hands kneaded at a lump of too-sticky dough. Frazzled eyes connected with his through blonde hair that fell from her lopsided bun.

"Problems?"

He tried hard to keep the humor from his voice, but her glare said he'd failed. Ever since they'd stayed the handful of days at the parsonage and the weeks they'd been in their new home, Klara had been trying to learn the new recipes Betty had taught her. Some turned out delicious. Most left Klara grumpy or weepy. Sometimes both.

Granted, the emotions might be due to Klara being pregnant.

Betty connecting the dots had left both Klara and Otto whirling, but for once, the whirling was a good thing.

Klara would be an incredible mother. Though the prospect of more responsibility would've terrified him a few months ago, Otto looked forward to being a father with eager anticipation.

He crossed the room, wrapped his arms around Klara so her back pressed against his front, and nuzzled her neck. She huffed but leaned her head sideways to give him better access. He spread his hands wide across her flat belly, looking forward to when it would be large with child. He wouldn't be telling her that, not with how she'd been jumping from one emotion to the next like a newborn lamb.

He pressed another kiss to her neck, then slid his hands to her elbows and lifted her hands from the dough. Sticky white clung to all her fingers and caked her hands all the way up to her wrists. A clump of dough plopped into the mess on the table, and Klara growled in frustration.

"I think maybe the dough won the battle this time." He couldn't hold in the chuckle any longer.

Klara jabbed her elbow back into his ribs, but the lack of force and shake of her shoulders in laughter belied the action. He stepped around her, adjusting his grip on her arms, and led her to the washbasin. He wagged his eyebrows at her. She rolled her eyes in answer.

He plunged their hands in the lukewarm water and slowly ran his fingers along her skin to clean the goop off. The bright red of her just-healed burns that matched his own put a lump in his throat. He'd come so close to losing her—to losing them both. The reminder of the fire still overwhelmed him at times.

He still wasn't sure what he thought about the men

responsible for so much pain dying in a shootout with the marshal. Yes, he was thankful that they could no longer hurt people, but part of him wished they'd suffered in their punishment. He inhaled the scent of flour clinging to Klara's hair and exhaled his anger. It had no place in his life anymore.

Lifting her clean hand to his lips, he kissed each new scar softly. She cupped his cheek with her free hand. He took her hand still held in his and pressed it flat to his pounding heart. Her head tipped back and her eyes closed as her face relaxed into an expression of joy.

Dear Lord, she was beautiful.

And she was all his.

Otto swung her into his arms, eliciting an airy gasp from her. She pressed her face into his neck, planting feathery kisses on his skin. His smile stretched across his face as he took the stairs to their bedroom two at a time. Who could've guessed that he'd go to town one morning for flour and bacon and come home with a wife?

Want more historical western romance chockfull of suspense and romance? Need more Trapper Dan antics? Check out the Vestige in Time series for adventures that will keep you on the edge of your seat.

ALSO BY SARA BLACKARD

<u>Vestige in Time Series</u>
Vestige of Power
Vestige of Hope
Vestige of Legacy
Vestige of Courage

<u>Stryker Security Force Series</u>
Mission Out of Control
Falling For Zeke
Capturing Sosimo
Celebrating Tina
Crashing Into Jake
Discovering Rafe
Convincing Derrick
Honoring Lena

<u>Alaskan Rebels Series</u>
A Rebel's Heart
A Rebel's Beacon
A Rebel's Promise
A Rebel's Trust

<u>Wild Hearts of Alaska</u>
Wild about Denali
Wild about Violet

Wild about Rory

Hearts of Roaring Fork Valley

Flight of a Wild Heart

Song of a Determined Heart

ABOUT THE AUTHOR

Sara Blackard is an award-winning romance novelist who writes stories that thrill the imagination and strum heartstrings. When she's not crafting wild adventures and romances that make readers swoon, she's homeschooling her four adventurous boys and one fearless princess, keeping their off-grid house running (don't ask if it's clean), or enjoying the Alaskan lifestyle she and her Hunky Hubster love. Visit her website at www.sarablackard.com

Made in the USA
Monee, IL
09 November 2024